Rufe eased the double-barrels around into sight. Someone saw them, squawked like a wounded eagle, and men scattered every which way except for a grizzled, hard-looking old cattleman, and all he did was lean down upon the tie rack flintily staring back. He hardly more than raised his voice when he said: "What the hell you figure to do with that silly thing, cowboy? It don't have a range of over a hunnert and fifty feet." He spat, then said: "You better come out of there. So far, you ain't done nothing that maybe should have been done long ago. You shoot anyone else, and that's going to make a heap of difference, so you'd better just walk out of there."

Rufe listened, and pondered, then called back: "I got a better idea, mister, *you* come inside!"

The old stockman chewed, spat, looked left and right where the wary crowd was beginning to creep up again, then he said: "All right, I'll come inside. But I got to warn you…"

FEUD ON THE MESA

Lauran Paine

LEISURE BOOKS NEW YORK CITY

A LEISURE BOOK®

October 2008

Published by special arrangement with Golden West Literary Agency.

Dorchester Publishing Co., Inc.
200 Madison Avenue
New York, NY 10016

ISBN 10: 0-8439-6034-5
ISBN 13: 978-0-8439-6034-1

The name "Leisure Books" and the stylized "L" with design are trademarks of Dorchester Publishing Co., Inc.

Printed in the United States of America.

10 9 8 7 6 5 4 3 2 1

Visit us on the web at www.dorchesterpub.com.

FEUD ON THE MESA

TABLE OF CONTENTS

Renegades Beat the War Drum. 1

Texas Herds Bring Death. 45

Feud on the Mesa. 93

Renegades Beat the War Drum

I

The words were thick with fury and scorn: "Injun lover! Squawman!"

Caleb Doorn only shrugged with a saturnine, dour smile on his face. "Not by a damned sight, *hombre*. I think you've laid the blame where it don't fit."

The freighter, whiskey-red eyes aglow with anger, sneered at the buckskin-clad frontiersman in front of him. "I reckoned you'd feel thataway. Look at you." The bitter, muddy eyes swept over the lean, hard man before him. "Beaded moccasins, buckskin huntin' shirt, and fringed britches to match, like a redskin." A thick, grimy finger pointed accusingly at the sky-blue, beaded knife sheath with its inlaid beaded triangles in blue and white, and the heavy deer-horn handle.

He reached over and flipped the little twig at the bottom of the sheath, twisted into a circle and with a small, tightly stretched wisp of scalp hair dangling from it. "What kind of o' hair is that, Squawman? Injun or white? Ha, more'n likely it's white hair offen some woman or kid."

The man had worked himself into a killing frenzy and Doorn saw it. He didn't want to fight the man, especially since he was a stranger in Denton. The small bunch of other whiskey-flushed faces in the rude mud-wattle saloon were cold-eyed and menacing, too. He shrugged again. "That's Apache hair, pardner. The same kind of hair you're cussin' about right now."

"Y'damned liar!" The man was poised like a big, wobbly stag.

Doorn's face went bleak and his lips flattened over his teeth. "Keep back, freighter."

The words had a sobering effect on some of the spectators, but the belligerent freighter only sneered at them. He licked his lips and hunched forward a little.

Doorn saw it coming and raised himself slightly on the balls of his moccasin-clad feet. When the big man came in with a furious, obscene oath, he side-stepped quickly and lashed out with all the power of a whipcord, bone-and-sinew body. The freighter half turned, blundered up against the bar with a room-shaking jar, shook his head foggily, and straightened up.

"Forget it, mister."

It was a useless warning. The freighter came in again, more wobbly than ever, his breath whistling through his tobacco-stained teeth like the fetid wind from a stagnant marsh. He lashed out with a massive, oak-like arm. Doorn dropped to one knee, rolled his shoulder, and the blow tore into the man's unprotected midriff like a battering ram. The freighter went down with a gasping sob.

Doorn was coming back to his feet, his hand dropping instinctively to his .44. He was ready for the others that he knew, from a lifetime spent on the frontier, would be rushing him, when a deep, edgy voice broke in. "None o' that, damn ya. Your friend got just what he come a-lookin' fer."

Doorn looked back and saw the short, massive bartender, a worn and shiny wagon spoke in one brawny hand, standing, spraddle-legged, behind the mob of snarling freighters, drovers, and scouts who were edging in on Doorn.

"One at a time, boys." The words were silky soft, and the hard-eyed men hesitated, hung back, then slowly straightened up and moved back toward the bar, grumbling to themselves and throwing venomous glances at the man in buckskin.

The ugly, pockmarked bartender, a sprinkling of pale gray through the jet-black, coarse hair of his bullet-shaped head, glared at his customers and resumed where he had left off mopping up the puncheon bar top with a sticky, damp rag.

"I know how you feel. Ain't a wagon or a cow been able to move outen Denton since the 'Paches took up the knife. Wal"—he wagged his head slowly, somberly—"they's a lot o' truth in what this here stranger says. The whites is mad because they can't do no business what with Injuns keepin' the town cut off. Sure, it hurts my trade, too. Hell, most o' you boys been bottled up here for a month, an' your business with me's been mostly credit business. I don't like that no more than you do. But when this here *hombre* says the whites are makin' heroes out of themselves by puttin' out a fire they started themselves, he's plumb right." Again the big head bobbed up and down convincingly. "We come in here an' shoved the redskins out. That's what we call progress. I ain't sayin' we shouldn't've done it. Dammit, we had to. But then when the Injuns fight back, an' we gotta beat 'em off . . . well, dammit all, just like this feller says, we're only puttin' out a fire we started ourselves. That's plumb right, too, an' ain't no one got no call to try an' gang up on a man 'cause he speaks out after thinkin' things over. Not here in Jock Leclerc's saloon, the Southern Cross, no siree. Not by a damned sight."

One of the cattle drovers, a tall, lean, thin-faced man with pensive, sad eyes, cleared his throat. "I allow there's somethin' to what you say at that." He tossed his head a little under the hard, stiff brim of his low-crowned hat. "I'm sorry, stranger, reckon it's the eternal waitin' an' knowin' that a bunch of cattle are eatin' ya into bankruptcy, while them troops are supposed to be comin' up to clear the redskins offen the desert so's a man can move on again."

Doorn flashed a rare, shy grin at the big man and nodded. "My fault, too, I reckon. Shouldn't've said anythin'."

The freighter began to moan and the bartender went around and poured half a water glass full of green whiskey down his throat. The man jerked up to a sitting position with a strangled oath and sprayed the acid-like liquor half across the room. Someone laughed, and others took it up. The tension was broken. The freighter got unsteadily to his feet, white-faced and beaded with nauseous sweat. He held onto the bar next to Doorn, gagged eloquently a couple of times, raised his head, looked straight into Doorn's eyes, blanched a little, and forced up a very ill-looking, lopsided grin. "Gawd, *hombre*, what'd you hit me with?"

The laughter was explosive and the bartender, even, white teeth flashing sympathetically, released his hold on the wagon spoke under the bar. Doorn ordered another drink for the man and the episode was closed, but Caleb had learned one thing. Denton was nerve-raw and red-eyed after a month of being cut off from the rest of the frontier by the Apache cordon. It was better to say nothing than to argue.

Just before Jock Leclerc closed his rude saloon for the night, an old, wizened barfly was staring with watery eyes into the amber liquid on the bar in front of him. He and Leclerc were the only ones left in the saloon and the bartender was watching the customer sip his rotgut whiskey with an impatient, jaundiced eye.

The oldster screwed up his bloated face and spoke softly. "I seen him somewhere, I dang' well know it, but I can't recollect where."

"Who?"

"That there scout with the Kiowa Apache scalpin' knife that whupped that there freighter this afternoon."

The bartender said nothing and finished wiping up the last of the strong smelling, sticky tin cups. He turned abruptly, his day's labors completed.

Before he could speak, however, the old man slammed down his mug with an oath. "Now I recollect. He's Caleb Doorn."

The bartender leaned heavily on the backbar and frowned at the oldster with a critical look. "Y'sure?"

"Yep, shore as shootin'. I was in Santa Fé when he was court-martialed an' drummed offen the post for refusin' to lead a squadron o' cavalry inter a Comanche ambush." The old head wagged on its scrawny neck. "Army called it insubordination, whatsoever that means. Anyway, they run him offen the post, yes siree."

The bartender shifted his weight a little and looked, long and steadily, at the old fellow without seeing. Caleb Doorn was a name to conjure with. An ex-soldier who had refused to leave the frontier after his disgrace and had mingled with Indians and whites indiscriminately ever since. There were almost incredible legends of his feats with a .44 and his big scalping knife with its weighted, forked, deer-horn handle.

He nodded thoughtfully. Yes, that would be Doorn all right. He'd level a foe with a knee-dropped uppercut into the belly like that. Well, he had seemed to be every bit as good a man as the frontier stories made him out to be. Leclerc yawned prodigiously and looked at the triangular little piece of gold coin that the old man had left on the bar. He pocketed it owlishly, swabbed out the tin mug, and took off his apron with another big yawn.

Dawn was a chilly pink mist on the horizon when Jock Leclerc came out of his back room, puffy-eyed and sober-faced, and lifted down the big door bar. He started slightly when he opened the doors to look at the clear, pale sky, which was a habit contracted in his youth when a hint about the weather told him more than he needed to know now. He blinked rapidly at the lean, fresh-eyed man leaning indolently against the hitch rail, a big black horse, saddled and with full saddlebags, behind him.

" 'Mornin'."

Doorn nodded with a wisp of a grin in his eyes. He had seen Leclerc's quick start at seeing him standing there. " 'Mornin'. Can a man get a little breakfast with you before he leaves Denton?"

Leclerc started to say something, hesitated, and nodded. "Sure, come on an' I'll whip up a little fried meat. Ain't eaten yet myself."

Doorn was relaxed on a hard, hand-hewn bench against the shadowy north wall of the hovel when Leclerc came out of the back room with two huge, thick platters of greasy food. Somehow—probably through much practice—he managed to hold two steaming hot tin mugs of deep brown tea without spilling.

Arranging the victuals with a calm, ham-like paw, Leclerc sighed heavily and dropped onto the bench across from Doorn, who was eating with a patent hunger. "Leavin' Denton, right now . . . an' especially alone . . . is pretty risky business." Leclerc sprayed a thick mist of pepper over his food as he spoke, without looking up.

Doorn nodded briefly. "I reckon. Still, I came in here yesterday alone an' no one bothered me. No one, that is, that had a red skin."

It was an oblique reference to the belligerent freighter and Leclerc smiled. "He didn't mean nothin'. Just a case o' bein' cooped up too long." Leclerc tried to act casually when next he spoke. "Got a destination, this trip?"

"Yep. Goin' to see old Red Sleeves an' see what I can do about gettin' your siege lifted."

"Damn! Them hostiles'll massacree ya." He wagged his head solemnly. "It ain't that important. The soldiers'll be along one o' these days."

Doorn looked up for the first time, and shook his head. "No, I don't think so. Y'see, that's what brought me down here in the first place. I was scoutin' fer a detachment of dragoons out o' Lauder. They were whipped and driven back by a big confederacy of Apaches . . . Tontos, Chiricahuas, Mescaleros, Tres Piños, and the rest." At Leclerc's wide-eyed stare, Doorn shrugged. "So, ya see, this is more than a few irate bucks thirstin' for hair and loot. It's a carefully organized confederacy of Southwestern Apaches making their big holy war against the *ojos claros*, the pale eyes."

"Well, I'll be damned. Never thought they had it in 'em."

"You know 'em?"

Leclerc shrugged eloquently and resumed his eating. "Used to trap an' trade with 'em. Matter of fact, this here saloon used to be a tradin' post until the freighters started comin' by here regular, then I went in for rotgut instead of trade goods. More ready money an' steadier customers. Less tension, too. Never could depend on them Injuns. Might come an' trade today, then not show up again for a year." He stuffed his mouth, and leaned back thoughtfully. "But I never thought they had the brains to join together in their fightin'."

Doorn pushed away his empty plate. "To tell the truth, I never did, either. In fact, the main reason I'm goin' over to 'em is to see if an idea I've got is right . . . about this here uprisin'."

"What idea?"

"I figure it's Mexicans or whites behind this thing. Maybe gunrunners or dishonest traders buyin' their loot." He arose and dug into a small pocket in the wide hem of his hunting shirt.

Leclerc guessed the frontiersman's intentions and shook his head firmly. "Ferget it. We just had breakfast together." Doorn looked down at him and hesitated. "When you come back, if you do, stop in an' let me know whether your idee is right or not, an' we'll call it square on the breakfast."

II

The sun was coming lazily over the shrouded mountains, far to the east, by the time Caleb Doorn's big, sleek black horse was a small speck in the drowsing prairie that faced north and east from Denton. He knew the Southwestern Indians as well as anyone on the frontier and was confident that he had not gone unnoticed by beady black eyes that kept a constant vigil on Denton.

It was anyone's guess where Red Sleeves's camp was. It moved often and abruptly—partly through necessity, and partly through a restlessness that was typical of the short, powerful Apache chieftain. Caleb figured he'd meet his man soon enough, if he just kept riding into the known heartland of the Apache *ranchería*. The sun was directly overhead, a molten mass of purgatorial heat, when two slow-riding, vividly painted braves bisected his path. Doorn stopped, relaxed, and waited. They slowed to a walk and came on, faces livid in red and black war colors and their short, husky bodies burned almost black by the blasting sun.

Doorn saw many things as the Apaches came up, watching him with unblinking eyes, their hands curled handily around short, heavy Sharps carbines. Their horses were sweat-stained and a little gaunt, but still fat. Stolen horses, settlers' horses, more than likely. Both of the hostiles had a nap of scalps swinging gently at their belts, along with .44 pistols and the ever-present knives. The painted symbols indicated that the older of the two was a renowned warrior, while the younger was a novice.

They stopped about twenty feet from Doorn, having studied him as they came on. They observed only the briefest silence, demanded by protocol, before the elder—a man Doorn's own age—spoke. His eyes were broodingly venomous and his splendid form was corded with knotty hard muscles that had a liberal sprinkling of battle scars. He spoke Spanish, mother tongue of the old Southwest: "*¿Qué dice, ojo claro? ¿Como se va?*"

Doorn looked directly into the other's eyes and let a silent moment slip by before he answered in English. He affected not to understand Spanish, in accordance with a plan that he'd formulated as he rode. "I'm looking for a great Apache called Red Sleeves."

The warrior frowned slightly and looked inquiringly at the younger man. This one couldn't have been over nineteen or twenty years old; he had a smooth, round, pudgy face and a lean, tough body not yet filled out with the muscles and weight of maturity. The younger brave, still looking at Doorn with curiosity, interpreted. The older man threw a quick, scornful smile at Doorn and spoke to the younger man, who smiled triumphantly and nodded dryly. "We will take you to the *ranchería*. Come."

Doorn nodded pleasantly and rode with the Indians, who maintained a distance of about ten feet between the white man's horse and their own. The ride was a silent one, although the attitude of the younger man was clearly one of curiosity.

Finally, as they neared a pine-scented pass that led into the dense growth of a low, rolling nest of verdant foothills, the young man spoke again. "What are you called?"

"Silent Outcast."

The name had an instantaneous affect on the buck. He looked up, quick and startled, turned to his companion, and grunted in guttural Apache. The older man reined in closer and looked hard at Doorn. He spoke in Spanish again and the novice interpreted in a voice tinged with respect.

"That is No Salt, my uncle. I am Free Man. No Salt asks if you were with the yellowlegs we fought at Bitter Springs and drove back to Fort Lauder?"

"Yes, I was guiding them to Denton. When they fell back, I slipped away in the darkness, and rode to Denton."

No Salt listened to the interpretation with an intense look, gave a throaty, deep grunt of admiration. He had heard of Silent Outcast, the white warrior who had been disowned by the other whites—for what reason the Indians neither knew nor cared—and he felt the honor of riding with such a renowned warrior.

"*¿No habla español?*" It was a sincere and earnest question. No Salt felt humiliation at having to talk to such a great fighting man through the mouth of a second person, and especially one so inexperienced and unproven as his nephew. Doorn shrugged indifferently and looked at the younger man. Free Man shrugged and remained silent, aware of the purpose behind his uncle's question.

The Apache encampment was a sprawling, primitive splash of vivid color in a secluded meadow. Doorn was amazed at the size of it. There were teepees, mud-daubed branch hogans like the Navajos make, crude brush shelters with skins tossed indifferently over them, and plain, open camp areas where weapons and personal belongings were strewn around on the trampled buffalo grass, or hanging listlessly from thick growths of chokecherry bushes. The horse herd, visible on another clearing through a thin screen of stately firs and pines, was huge. Indifferent herdsmen lounged beside horses with their heads down while watching the remuda graze in the tall, succulent meadow grass.

There was a quiet buzzing, intermingled with shrill oaths as squaws chased mangy, half-wild and sly dogs away from the cooking fires and stew pots. Now and then loud laughter would peal over the humming sound of the big camp, and the screams of children at play rode the afternoon air like a nostalgic benediction. No Salt motioned to Free Man, who swung away with a disappointed look and rode listlessly toward the camp of his people. The older warrior then motioned Doorn to follow him, and they threaded their way through the maze of Indian camps until they dismounted before a brush lodge set a little apart from the others. No Salt importantly waved up a couple of young boys and growled succinctly at them. Each sprang forward and took the horses' reins, big-eyed and staring at the white man.

Inside the cool, shady brush hut, Red Sleeves and three older men sat in stony-faced silence, looking at Caleb, as No Salt recited his meeting with the frontiersman. Red Sleeves motioned to the ground and Caleb sat, as did No Salt. Red Sleeves had been educated by a missionary and spoke good English, although he was not known to have any sympathies with the whites. "We know of you, Silent Outcast."

It was neither a welcome nor a condemnation. The chief was waiting to hear Doorn's purpose in coming into his camp before he passed judgment.

"I am honored, although I am sad, too," Doorn said.

"We all are sad." Red Sleeves spoke in a distrustful voice.

"The Apaches fought the soldiers a few days back and beat them," Doorn reminded.

The chieftain was a shrewd man. "Is that why you are sad? Because the Apaches whipped the *ojos claros?*"

"Yes, but my sadness comes from more than a victory or a defeat. It comes from my knowledge that the Apaches are fighting against something they can never conquer."

"This," said Red Sleeves, his eyes alive and hot, "is not the kind of a war you know, Silent Outcast. This is a great and righteous war, this is the kind of a war David fought with the enemies of the Mighty Host."

Doorn recognized the missionary's teachings and wondered how they could be so twisted. He nodded as though in agreement, and Red Sleeves's face lost some of its impassiveness. "You believe, then?"

"In part, yes. In part, no."

"You speak a riddle."

"No, Red Sleeves. I speak the mystic teachings of the Great Ones." From the looks on their faces, two of the older men, sitting motionless and vacant-faced, as well as No Salt, didn't understand the exchange of words at all. But the other man, about Red Sleeves's own age, very dark with a hairline that left almost no forehead at all, unpainted like the others, was following the conversation with keen interest. Doorn knew he understood.

"But the Great Ones say we have been wronged."

"True, Red Sleeves. True. But the Apaches would have to number in the millions, not the hundreds and thousands, to avenge that wrong."

Red Sleeves was plainly perplexed. "You agree that the Indian has been wronged, so you think like we do, but you don't think he can avenge himself. What do you think the Indian should do, then?"

"Learn to live in this world that has always been his but which is changing now, by learning the ways of the new life. Learn to farm, to labor, to sew and build. Do all this in peace with the whites. Study their way and profit from it," Doorn said.

Red Sleeves's eyes were hard and cold now. "No! The Indian is a free man. He does not imprison the ground in little fields by putting fences around them. He does not kill off the humpback and the antelope, so that he must bring in his own cattle and nurse them. He does not tear up the earth and smooth it out again, and plant grass where the Great Ones had already planted grass. The Indian is no slave. He is a free man. He does not want to live as the *ojos claros* live. It is better that he should die than to be a slave."

Doorn sat for a long moment in perfect, grave-faced silence. Red Sleeves's outburst left him fiery-eyed and breathing hard. He faced his councilors and launched forth into a violent harangue, in Apache, spitting and snarling words from his chest in a gurgling staccato of anger.

No Salt and two elders, who apparently didn't understand English, grunted and cast baleful glances at Doorn. The unpainted man with the low forehead was smiling in a triumphant, lazy way. When Red Sleeves had stopped his tirade, this man's voice, soft and clear, came into the conversation in perfect English. Caleb was startled. "Your memory is poor, Caleb Doorn. You don't recall El Lobo, the Taos *Comanchero*."

The swarthy face was smiling expectantly. Doorn recognized him then. Sam Ginn, one of that reckless, unscrupulous brotherhood of white and mixed-blood traders who were called *Comancheros*, or roaming traders. Some were honest, fearless men, but most were men who took the big gamble for a quick and rich profit. Of these latter, Sam Ginn was known as a half-breed Comanche, from the Mexican territory that became Texas a little later. Here was a shrewd trader, waxing rich and safe where other, more decent men were leaving their bones to bleach under the savage, hot sun of the untamed land. Caleb had met Ginn before; he had ordered him off the base at Santa Fé several times. There was no respect or friendship here.

He inclined his head softly, a pensive, accusing light in his deep-set, gray eyes. "Sam, I thought it must be something like this. I figured someone must have stirred them up . . . someone who had an ability to organize and profiteer."

Ginn shrugged indifferently, the cool smile still on his heavy face. "I don't profiteer. Sell them a little powder, a few cases of contraband whiskey and bullets, trade for horses and jewelry of the whites they kill." His shoulders rose and fell agreeably, leisurely. "Better I get it than it rot on the desert. Good business, Doorn, that's all. Good business."

Doorn motioned toward the Apache *n'deh b'keh* moccasins, the breechclout, and the scalping knife. "Playin' Indian, Sam, so's you won't be caught by the soldiers and shot for a renegade?"

"*Seguro*. That's good business, too, ain't it?" Ginn asked.

Doorn turned to Red Sleeves, who was listening to the conversation. "You are making a mistake by letting this man talk up a war. He is a renegade. The Apaches do not like traitors any more than the whites do. This man. . . ."

Red Sleeves slashed the air with an impatient arm. "He is advisor to the Apaches. He brings us the things we need." He shrugged indifferently. "He is well paid, but, as he has said, the trinkets we pay him with are of little value to us. It is a good trade."

"Red Sleeves, you are bringing down fire and the sword on your own people. This man has talked you into a great wrong."

"I don't want to hear any more, Silent Outcast."

Sam Ginn turned languidly to the chief. "Let's take him on the raid with us tonight. It would be well if his corpse was found among the dead whites at Clearwater Springs." The smile was full of hate now and the small, bird-like black eyes were cruel pools of resentment. "We would have the last laugh. The white soldiers would find him left behind by the Apaches and would think he was, indeed, a renegade . . . like they said he was when they drummed him out of their army at Santa Fé."

For a long, brooding moment Red Sleeves thought over Ginn's plan. He respected the fighting *ojo claro* before him, but this was a war to extinction and the great white fighters were no better than the lesser ones. In fact, it would be well to kill the great ones first, then the Indians would have nothing but pale-faced human sheep to slaughter.

Red Sleeves nodded slowly, looking straight into Caleb's eyes. "Yes, we will take him with us and leave his body among the dead. But the Apaches shall kill him, for he is a brave warrior and no stain must linger after the death of great fighting men." He turned to No Salt: "Guard him well, No Salt, until we are ready to ride."

III

No Salt was a good guardian. The day was almost spent and he took his prisoner over to his own camp to eat. The meal was a dolorous, silent affair with Free Man eating desultorily, No Salt chewing in carefully averted grimness, and No Salt's squaw impassive and dour. Caleb Doorn ate hungrily. The food wasn't tasty, and Doorn knew better than to ask what it was. It was the first meal since he had left Leclerc at Denton. His mind was busy, too. The Apaches had not disarmed him and he resolved, once in the neighborhood, to fire his gun and let the settlers at Clearwater Springs know that trouble was coming. That he'd die, he understood, but he was to die anyway.

No Salt wiped his hands painstakingly on the uppers of his moccasins. "You are to leave your gun and knife with me."

Doorn felt his hopes tumble. He considered immediate resistance but decided against it. Free Man had interpreted again and was watching the frontiersman owlishly. Doorn spoke as he unbuckled the wide, mahogany-colored belt and let his .44 and scalping knife drop gently against the warm earth. "One more gun and knife to hasten the fall of my brothers."

Free Man bristled. "It is not so."

"Yes, the result of warfare is warfare. The Apaches have been my brothers, and I hate to see them used," Doorn said angrily.

"No one uses the Apaches."

"Not even Sam Ginn?"

"No. Sam Ginn is a 'breed Comanche. He is like one of us, his race fights the *ojos claros*, too," Free Man answered.

Caleb nodded thoughtfully as he watched the shadows lengthen. "Yes, one half of him fights the *ojos claros*, while the other half profits from the fighting. It is a good combination, for a trader."

No Salt requested an interpretation, listened with downcast eyes and furrowed brow as Free Man told him what Caleb had said, looked oddly at the frontiersman, and arose, growling an order that was quickly made plain to Doorn. The time had come to ride.

A raucous turmoil boiled through the large Indian encampment as the warriors, uniformly short, bandy-legged, and heavy-shouldered, painted and decorated in lurid symbols of death and ruin, assembled on their horses. They were awaiting the arrival of their war leaders, Red Sleeves and a dry-eyed, fanatically featured younger man called Antonio—a kidnapped Navajo who had grown up as an Apache.

Caleb looked over the fighting bucks. He estimated their number at 400—more Apaches than he had ever seen in a fighting party before.

Red Sleeves rode up beside him and inclined his head respectfully, broodingly. "There are fool Apaches just as there are fools among the *ojos claros*. The Apache fools would have you die in disgrace." He shook his head firmly. "This will not happen,

Silent Outcast. The older warriors know you are a great fighting man. They will see that you die as one. There shall be no shame to follow your spirit."

Caleb nodded gravely, his face a blank painting. The Indian turned his horse, cast a careful eye over the gathered multitude of fighters, delayed the departure for a dramatic moment while all eyes were upon him, looked briefly heavenward, then nodded. The quiet of a moment before was broken by shrill shrieks from the children and women, the deep-chested, savage screams of the eager marauders, and the spiteful cries of the older men who had to remain behind. The grass was churned under 1,600 unshod hoofs, and a strong smell of animal and human sweat followed the disturbed atmosphere as the hostile bucks rode gracefully away from their *ranchería* without a backward glance. They talked and gesticulated among themselves, already forgetting home and families, to brag about the things they would do when they came to Clearwater Springs.

The darkness came down swiftly and with it a thick sickle of a moon that cast an eerie, ghostly light over the great sweep of the broad landscape. Sage, pungent with the yellow flowers blooming profusely in the late spring, and thorny chaparral, gray-green in the watery light, were a fitting, weird backdrop for the wild throng of horsemen who rode briskly toward their objective.

Caleb let his mind wander back to previous visits to Clearwater Springs. He fixed the location of the log and mud general store, squatty and forbidding. The clutch of shacks hastily thrown athwart the dusty trail that wound past the clear, cold spring that bubbled out of the hard ground. He recalled the scattering of emigrant soddies out on the

prairie. The sober, big-eyed children and the worn,
patient women with their lean, stubborn, husbands
in homespun. Clearwater Springs was a struggling
settlement, where hardship and suffering were in
the warp of everyone's life. Drought, howling winters, illness without remedies, and accidents without help were the accepted lots of existence. Even
so, Clearwater Springs was coming up out of the
sordidness of its creation by stubborn insistence on
the part of the settlers. Now it was to be shattered,
fired, and devastated, which was tragic—but all
this was to be laid waste for no better reason than
because Sam Ginn, the *Comanchero*, wanted to hawk
the pathetic treasures of forlorn people and make a
profit.

Red Sleeves rode back to where Doorn was riding
erectly between No Salt, and Free Man. He reined
up beside the white man, and Caleb noticed that another Indian was with him. He nodded and the warrior nodded back. He jutted his chin toward the
other man. "Antonio."

Caleb nodded to the younger man, who ignored
the greeting and looked at the frontiersman with bitter hatred in his harsh, twisted features. Caleb swung
his eyes back to Red Sleeves. "Clearwater Springs
isn't far ahead." The Apache nodded again but said
nothing. "Sam Ginn should make a good profit from
your work tonight."

At this, Antonio looked quickly at Doorn. He
spoke in a deep, husky voice. "We are not without
friends."

Doorn shrugged indifferently. "No. You'll have
Sam Ginn for a friend so long as you do the fighting
and bring the loot to him."

Antonio's black eyes sparkled in their muddy

settings, and he showed his white, even teeth in a snarl. "You lie!"

Doorn's comeback was swift and biting. "In your teeth!" he said.

Antonio was surprised and infuriated. He swore a blasting oath in Spanish and yanked his horse toward Caleb, drawing his knife as he went. Red Sleeves jumped his horse in between them and roared at Antonio who, ignoring his companion in his demonic fury, pushed closer. Doorn was watching like a hawk but he made no move to get away from the wild Apache. Other warriors, hearing the violent oath, came wraith-like out of the shadows and watched the drama of anger that seethed in their midst.

Red Sleeves forced his horse in harder and frowned savagely at Antonio. He spoke in English, which was not generally understood by the other Apaches. "Silent Outcast must not die yet. The council has agreed that he is to be left at Clearwater Springs."

Antonio, beside himself, swore obscenely at Red Sleeves, whose blunt jaw jutted dangerously and made a brief, thunderous tirade in Apache to which Red Sleeves nodded grimly. "Yes. He will die. It has been decided on. But you will not kill him here."

Antonio was subsiding a little. The first crazy red mist before his eyes had paled a little as he looked balefully at the captive and holstered his knife with an exasperated movement. Doorn taunted him again and this time Red Sleeves, afraid the fight might erupt into a sectional battle then and there, told him to be silent. Caleb looked thoughtfully at Red Sleeves as an outrider came back and told them that the lights of the springs were up ahead.

"Red Sleeves, you are a smart man, if your friend is not. You are letting the Apaches be made into tools to enrich that renegade, Sam Ginn. I warn you. Whether I live or die, the *ojos claros* will pursue you to the end of your world, and wipe you out if you attack this settlement." He raised his hands, palms upwards in an earnest plea. "You are not of *los viejos*, the old veterans of the yesterdays. You can learn the new way. Don't lead the Apaches to their doom."

Red Sleeves had long had a suspicion, although he had never voiced it. Now, with the crossroads of his race in his hands, he looked hard at Doorn with a puzzled frown. "We are a persecuted race. We have been robbed. Our lands. . . ."

Doorn interrupted impatiently as he saw the bucks fanning out before the foremost of the outlying sod houses up ahead. "You need not explain to me. I know all the wrongs the *ojos claros* have brought to you and your people. I know of more wrongs than you. But you do not help them by raiding. Besides, the Apaches have not the strength. . . ."

Antonio screamed wildly, savagely, deeply from his broad, bronze chest and the hellish scourge of the plains was unleashed. It was too late. Caleb locked his jaws in fierce grimness. Then this was to be a pyre of hate, and he was to lie in it, food for coyotes and red-eyed buzzards. He nodded his head in acceptance of his fate. This must have eventually happened, he thought. His life was forfeit on the frontier and his destiny was bound up inextricably with the wild, sullen land. All right, then he would die fighting.

Red Sleeves was hunching his muscles for the forward leap of his horse, going to join the others in their attack. Rifles and wild, despairing screams were pitting the watery light that bathed the eerie land when Caleb acted. His big black horse leaped like an animated battering ram under the viciousness of his heels and struck Red Sleeves's mount sideways. The Apache went down in a mêlée of thrashing arms and legs and flailing hoofs. Stunned by the fall, confused and bewildered, Doorn's fist found a ready target and the Apache relaxed from the blow.

Caleb, hearing the outraged screams of his guards, grabbed up a knife, pistol, and stubby carbine from the fallen warrior, turned in time to club No Salt from his horse with the rifle butt. He ducked under Free Man's poorly directed knife, clubbed the boy unconscious. Leaping to the back of his plunging black horse, Doorn flung the cracked rifle into the faces of three more incredulous braves who were coming in at him.

It all happened so fast, amid the howling pandemonium that marked Indian warfare and the desperate gunfire of the defenders in the soddies, that Doorn was running madly through the night before the pursuit put up a cry.

The quiet, somber night was suddenly alive. The first soddy was overrun and gutted, almost before its defenders knew what fury had descended upon them. The second and third outlying ranches were swamped, looted, and devastated in the same terrible, furious rush of Apaches out of the night. Rifle fire and blood curdling cries of the terrorized defenders came when they saw the enemy in among them.

Doorn rode like one possessed, trusting to the flying hoofs of his big black gelding to carry him through the myriad obstacles of refuse and equipment, firing his handgun as he went, and Clearwater Springs came hurriedly, tremblingly awake. At best, prepared and forewarned, the settlers were outnumbered about six or eight to one. But sleeping, unaware of the destruction that was hurtling toward them, there could be no defense of their homes and families.

Red Sleeves was mounted again, shaken and scratched and with a shooting ache in his head, but his pride was outraged more than his body. The news of Doorn's escape was carried quickly to Antonio, where he rode like a devil at the head of a maddened group of picked warriors. His muddy eyes blazed with scorn at Red Sleeves's failure, and he spun away from his fighting men to hunt the *ojo claro*.

Flames leaped at the attackers from the general store of Clearwater Springs. There were roars of angry pain in the night, evidence that the Apaches were paying a price. Red Sleeves launched two assaults against the log and mud building. They were successful in attaining their objective but could not force an entrance while the defending guns fired into them point-blank, leaving a welter of corpses. Red Sleeves was possessed of a monumental fury; his disgrace in losing the captive had changed him from a thoughtful, dignified man into a raging savage.

IV

Doorn stopped his blowing horse and the dull light glistened on the sweat-drenched coat. Orange tongues of flame were erupting against the black tapestry of the night. He saw that the mêlée had absorbed the Apaches and for the moment he was safe. Slowly he turned back. The night was a jumble of pandemonium and babble. A brave came trotting toward him, stiff-legged. Caleb raised his pistol, waited until the unsuspecting hostile was close, and fired. The Indian yanked up his horse, unbelieving. Doorn fired again and the man jerked upright, tottered, and went over sideways. Caleb caught the warrior's horse, stripped his own, and herded it beyond the village, re-saddled and mounted the Apache animal, and rode cautiously back into the night.

With nothing more than force of numbers, the attackers were flying through the darkness, assailing anything that promised a victim or loot. Many had found whiskey, and their hot blood—heated further by the raw spirits—turned them into demons. Caleb tied his new horse in a clump of brush at the edge of the creek and stalked among the attackers like a ghost. He came upon two young bucks looting a freighter's hastily deserted hovel. One of the bucks went down across the body of a small boy, and the other whirled to meet the unexpected attack. Doorn squeezed off another shot and the gun clicked dully on an empty casing. Hurling the gun in desperation, he rushed the warrior, knocked him down, and aimed a desperate kick at the gun hand that was swinging to bear on him. The brave howled in pain and dropped the gun. Caleb was astraddle the powerful form before the other could roll away, his knife rising and falling with quick, sure thrusts. The Apache struggled wildly and blood gushed from a hole in his stomach, and another in his chest. Doorn reversed the knife and swung it like an axe; the warrior relaxed, and Caleb leaped away. Picking up the gun the warrior had had, he disappeared in the half light.

Painted warriors slipped past in the night, their eyes glued to the stubbornly defended general store. Caleb went among them with the crouched, secretive grace of a puma. He saw Red Sleeves with a group of warriors around him. He waited, flat on the earth, for an opportunity to shoot or knife the leader, but had to give up since the braves continued to come in for instructions. Antonio was leaving the certain destruction of the embattled settlers to his fellows; he was searching for the captive who had antagonized him. The scalp of the Silent Outcast was worth more to Antonio than a hundred others.

Caleb was sneaking through the brush along the creekbed, toward his tethered Indian horse, when he heard someone skulking after him. He flattened in the moonlight and waited. It was a long wait, but eventually a ghostly form slithered into sight for a second, hesitated, listening, then came forward bent almost double, a pistol in one hand and a stained, slippery knife in the other. Doorn held his breath; Antonio had found him and was coming to settle with the frontiersman. Pushing gently against the cool earth, Doorn shoved himself erect and waited. Antonio came on without a sound. Caleb took a big breath and stepped out of the eerie night and confronted the startled Apache.

Antonio blinked rapidly, tensed a little, and his thin lips parted over the strong teeth. Doorn tossed caution to the wind and spoke musically in Spanish: "I should have shot you, killer of children and old women."

"Why didn't you, Silent Outcast?" Antonio straightened out of his crouch and looked triumphantly at the lighter, taller man with abiding scorn in his eyes.

"Because I want to kill you with my hands."

Antonio laughed softly. He had noticed that Doorn's gun was stuck into his waistband, while the knife was held loosely at his side. "I am here."

Doorn's first rush was a mistake and he knew it as the warrior side-stepped him. Antonio was grinning like a death's head now. He contemptuously dropped his pistol and began to circle. Doorn's face showed no fear or anger; he was impassive. The furious gunfire from the besieged village came down the cool night air to them and mingled with the gentler sound of the little creek behind them. Some ragged, unchecked tongues of flame leaped luridly into the night and cast wild, quivering light over the battleground. Doorn was conscious of the macabre scene around him as he watched the other working his way closer, knife extended and lying sideways in his corded fist.

Antonio leaped in and slashed cannily, aiming low. Caleb jumped back. He had not expected the leap, and felt the breath of the knife a fraction of an inch from his stomach. Again Antonio came in, carrying the fight to Doorn. Caleb affected to leap backward again, and the warrior, anticipating the maneuver, rushed him. It was a bad mistake and Antonio knew it when Doorn braced and dropped low, but his momentum wouldn't let him stop. He tried a half turn, but it was clumsy. Caleb's knife streaked in, straight as an arrow with the watery light reflecting sullenly off the blade. Antonio felt the slight burning sensation as the knife bit into the flesh over his hip. He jumped frantically away and turned. Caleb was following up his advantage and caught the Apache with his shoulder and upper left arm before Antonio could regain his balance. They crashed to the spongy earth together, Doorn on top.

Doorn used his knee liberally and heard the half choked-off, half agonized moan as Antonio's grip on his midriff slackened. Holding tightly, desperately to the slippery, lithe knife arm of the warrior, Caleb's knife rose high and descended twice. Antonio locked his jaw against the flood of gall and blood that swelled in his throat. His eyes were fanatically filming over in implacable hatred and Caleb slashed ragingly once more, and the quivering, sweaty body went limp.

Caleb, unheeding, heard the crescendo of the battle surging around the general store as he dragged Antonio's corpse into the brush. Unconsciously he knew that the few unfortunates, who had been unable to get to the store, had barricaded themselves in their hovels and had been killed.

Clarion clear in the cold predawn came the distant tones of a bugle. Caleb cocked his head incredulously. The closest soldiers were twenty-five miles away at

Fort Lauder. He heard far-off gunfire, like the popping of many small corks, and the fury on his sweaty, grimed, and weary face softened a little. It was unbelievable that the troops were coming, but that bugle call was unmistakable. A rumbling roar came from up by the general store. The warriors were being ordered back by Red Sleeves, and their angry growls were interspersed with the cries of the remaining defenders.

Caleb found his Indian horse and swung aboard. The air was cold now, and faint, weak light was outlining the wreckage and smoking ruins that cluttered the orderly landscape of what had been Clearwater Springs. He rode slowly through the tall brush and willows that lined the little creek. A band of retreating warriors splashed across the creek and thundered away toward the *ranchería*. Some carried bundles of loot for trade with Sam Ginn, who had stayed well out of rifle range during the fight, explaining that some of the defenders might recognize him. The braves were leaving before the troops could be seen. The bugle call and the rapid sound of premature firing had run them off. Doorn sat quietly in the saddle and watched them stream back over the rolling prairie. Some of the warriors were reeling in their saddles, others were swathed in crude bandages, some led riderless and stolen horses, while others rode exultantly, streams of scalps flying loosely from bridles, belts, and rifle barrels as they rode.

Caleb sat perfectly still and relaxed, as an unearthly silence settled over the settlement that only a few moments before had been washed over by savage screams and deafening gunfire. He looked up at the store; there was no sign of movement or life. He knew the defenders were standing, red-eyed and fearful, awaiting the next act in the drama. His eyes came slowly around to where the attackers were, a disorderly mob of small figures riding out of sight in the near distance.

Suddenly a movement caught his eye in the willows along the creek. He watched closely and saw a late brave, loaded with a tablecloth stuffed with loot, creep down to the creek, drink deeply, clamber awkwardly back onto his horse, and start out after his fellows. Doorn's gun came up slowly, carefully, and he tracked the jouncing marauder. The pistol's report was a belated, lonely sound in the dawn. The man's horse gave a tremendous leap, bucked insanely for a second or two, sending the startled warrior sprawling on the ground, surrounded by his scattered loot. Then the animal tore off, head high and nostrils distended, after the other Indian horses.

Doorn watched in surprise, concluding that his shot had missed the rider and had creased the horse. He shook out his own reins and splashed deliberately across the water, riding toward the brave, who was scrambling to his feet and jerking a battered six-gun out of the ragged folds of his breechclout. Doorn rode methodically at a walk until he saw the other's gun coming up, then he rammed his heels into the horse's sides and roared, careening forward.

The warrior fired and missed. He stood, spraddle-legged, and cocked his gun again. Caleb was within good shooting range, and his gun sounded loudly in his own ears as he shot at the squatty, indomitable figure before him. The brave refused to budge an inch and fired again. Caleb felt the quick, shocking, half numbness that goes with being shot. He was flying into the face of his enemy now, and his gun thundered three times in rapid succession. The hostile sagged, went down to his knees, and brought the gun up again. Caleb's horse hit him with stunning force before the shaking fingers could tighten on the trigger, and the warrior went over backward, blood gushing from his smashed face where the horse's knee had struck him solidly.

The brave's one true shot had struck Caleb in the leg below the knee, had glanced off the shin bone, and torn a jagged, gory hole in his right leg. He made up a tourniquet out of the dead man's headband, remounted, and rode back to Clearwater Springs.

Amid the acrid-smelling ruins of their settlement, a crowd of gaunt, red-eyed men and women were standing together with another group of grim-faced civilians. Caleb rode up somberly and they all turned to face him. He was surprised when Leclerc, the barman from Denton, stepped out of the mob and nodded at him. "It didn't work, did it?"

Caleb was tired and sore, but he understood that Leclerc was referring to Doorn's hope that he might be able to talk the hostiles into lifting their siege of Denton. He shook his head slowly. "No. Not only didn't work, but they brought me here to leave among the dead. Got away an' tried to give the alarm but"—he shrugged and looked at the carnage around him—"I'm afraid I didn't do much good." He looked at the motley, dry-eyed mob and frowned. "Where're the troops?"

Jock Leclerc shook his head harshly. "Ain't none. Your horse come into the livery barn at Denton last night, an' we figured what was up, got together all the freighters and drovers that've been bottled up in town fer the last month, an' backtracked him."

"But the bugle?"

"Trick. We wasn't strong enough to give 'em battle. They was a helluva lot of 'em, so we used the bugle to try a bluff, an' damned if it didn't work. They run like rabbits." His swarthy face was puzzled. "Where in hell'd they all come from?"

An older man went up beside Caleb's rapidly swelling leg and probed it. "Sit perfectly still," he said. Caleb nodded indifferently and the doctor went to work. "Leclerc, you recall a man named Sam Ginn?"

The saloon owner snorted. "Sure, he's one of the lowest *Comancheros* on the frontier. Troublemaker an' renegade o' the first water."

"He's talked Red Sleeves into forming a confederacy. He gets the loot and they get the revenge."

Jock Leclerc's features darkened under the rush of hot blood into his head. He bit down hard on the profanity that swelled in his throat. Suddenly his eyes came up hard and killing mad. "Can you ride?"

Doorn nodded without answering, frowning into the protesting eyes of the little doctor.

Jock Leclerc swung to the assembled, white-faced settlers. "Git your horses. If the soldiers won't do it, by Gawd we'll have to!" There were some murmurs among the people and a woman started hysterical, high moaning. Another woman led her away as the settlers fanned out, looking for something to ride. Caleb listened gravely to the little doctor, nodded, and frowned at the throbbing leg like he resented its interference in the job to be done.

Leclerc was on his horse and beside him. "We gotta do it now. They'll break their camp an' slope an' we'll never find 'em."

"I reckon."

"You can lead us to 'em?"

Caleb nodded. "How many men you got?"

"Not enough. Eighty or so come from Denton, and there must be about one or two hundred here."

Caleb's somber glance swept over the dulled, apathetic settlers who moved mechanically among the wreckage of their village. "There's about five hundred fightin' bucks in the *ranchería*, an' maybe two, three hundred more oldsters and youngsters handy."

Leclerc nodded thoughtfully. "I sent two men to Lauder fer the soljers last night. We'll leave scouts here at the springs an' at intervals out on the prairie to guide 'em in when they get here. They oughta make it no later than midday, if they travel fast."

Caleb's dour glance was matched with his words. "I reckon . . . if they've got fightin' officers instead of Eastern puppets."

Jock Leclerc looked over at him quickly, understood the brooding look and said nothing.

V

There weren't horses enough. What the attackers hadn't stolen had been shot. When the party left Clearwater Springs, there were no more than 250, all told. They left guides for the soldiers at regular intervals as they rode. This, too, cut down their effective striking force. The sun was getting a good start across the firmament in the new day when they encountered their first Apache vedette. They were fortunate in outriding and killing the warrior. However, two more braves fled at their approach and made it to the foothills before the hard-riding settlers could catch them.

Leclerc turned to Doorn and yelled against the whipping air that streamed past them: "They'll be ready now!"

Doorn nodded, white-faced and sunken-eyed.

Leclerc reined over closer. "Ride 'em down?"

Doorn looked around and shook his head vehemently: "Don't dare! Not enough of us. Have their route scouted an' try to ride far enough ahead of 'em to lay an ambush."

Leclerc wagged his head as they swept up the mountain pass into the fragrance of the pine and fir foothills below the Apache encampment. "Not a chance, they'll be watchin' us like hawks, now that they know we're comin'."

Doorn batted his eyes against the fuzziness that seemed to be eating at the edges of his mind. "Reckon you're right at that." He shrugged. "Whatever we do, tell the boys not to let the hostiles split 'em up. Stay together . . . everyone. If we get divided, we're goners."

Leclerc shouted the orders to stay together and they were relayed back down the charging host of riders. Somewhere, up ahead, a rifle cracked and a ragged volley answered. A moment later, Doorn looked down indifferently as he rode by, at the still, grotesquely sprawled body of a brave who had been shot out of a fir tree.

The excited, frenzied Apaches were breaking up their camp. They were in a broiling turmoil when scouts brought word to Red Sleeves that the settlers were coming. The hostiles were surprised that the pursuit was not made by soldiers, and Red Sleeves sent out a large body of warriors to try and find the soldiers he was certain were with the settlers. He feared a trick of some kind. Squaws were screaming at dogs and children and trying to load nervous, shying horses. There was a disorderly pandemonium throughout the camp that was only added to as the faint, unmistakable sound of a volley of firing stirred the feverish activity, each family trying to get away from the *ranchería* as quickly as the others. Much equipment was left behind as, inspired by Red Sleeves's worried face, all grabbed what was handy and fled. Scouts came and went and still no sign of the soldiers could be found.

Red Sleeves swore volubly in both Spanish and

English, the Apache tongue having no profanity in its vocabulary. He ordered out the warriors, recently returned from the springs, to hold off the settlers while the rest of the encampment tried to get away. In his perplexity, however, he ordered one half of the fighting men to go with the tribe. He felt certain that the soldiers were hidden in ambush.

The men under Doorn and Leclerc were brought to a sliding halt when they charged around a bend in the trail and came face to face with a furiously charging body of hostile horsemen. Shouts, curses, and gunfire welled up among the tall, stately trees as men, red and white, flung themselves off their horses and sought shelter. Jock Leclerc's roaring voice rumbled over the fight. He spurred his horse into the thickest of the fight and shot into the mass until his gun was empty, then he used a rifle for a club. The warriors were fighting defensively now, and the whiskey was turning to acid in their entrails.

Doorn, caught up in the zest of the moment, found a spring of inner energy somewhere and rode in behind Leclerc. A brave, resigned and doomed as the settlers swept in and past his tree stump defenses, jumped at Doorn, grabbed his wounded leg, and tried to pull him from the horse. A wild, sickening jolt of agony ran through the frontiersman and his pain-filled eyes were sharpened with a murderous lust as he reached down, his big pistol almost against the hostile's head, and pulled the trigger. Doorn straightened up as the settlers surged over the hostiles *en masse* and swept on up the trail into the Indian camp area.

The Apaches, who hadn't gotten away with their fellows, fought and died where they stood. The

settlers, flushed and maddened with their sufferings
and brief triumph, matched the hostiles in savagery
and abandon. Wounded warriors, spitting defiance
from the ground, were dispatched with knives and
rifle butts; the hectic skirmish was over almost as
quickly as it had begun. Doorn told Leclerc to keep
the settlers from following the main camp of Indians
through the treacherous forest, and, with a few exceptions, the attackers stayed back and hunted fugitives among the débris that littered the former
ranchería.

Doorn was getting painfully down from the Indian horse, before the abandoned brush hut of Red
Sleeves, when a single rifle shot echoed through the
noisy camp. Instantly everyone was hunting cover.
Caleb dropped flat as the bullet threw a violent gust
of gravel and dirt up beside him. He rolled toward
the abandoned shelter, drawing his pistol as he
went. Again the hidden gunman fired. This time the
bullet struck sideways on Caleb's pistol and ricocheted off into the air with a whine. Doorn dropped
the smashed gun and flexed his fingers, half numb
from the shock. He made it safely to the edge of a
small, fallen tree, floundered over it, and lay flat behind the punky, rotten trunk as the third shot flung
a gorge of splinters out of the wood.

The *ranchería* was deathly still as probing, narrowed
eyes and cocked guns sought the hidden gunman
among the brush and trees. Caleb had surmised
where his enemy was and began an oblique crawl,
knife in hand, through the foliage toward a flanking
spot. The silence was oppressive, and Doorn listened
with acutely sharpened instincts for a telltale sound
that would guide him. None came.

Somewhere, a long way off, a bugle call came distantly to the hidden settlers. Caleb heard with a tight smile and continued his crawl. He stopped his advance in a clump of chokecherry and sage. A movement off to his left and a little ahead had caught his eye. Cautiously he parted the brush and looked inquiringly among the shadows of the trees and his face froze into a thwarted grimace. Not 200 feet from where he was lying, Sam Ginn was turning a high-headed bay horse around, preparatory to mounting. Without a gun and with a leg that he knew would no longer support him, Caleb was forced to lie still and watch the renegade getting ready to escape.

Suddenly he cried out, involuntarily. Another figure, ghost-like and massive, shot up out of the brush almost at Ginn's feet and struck the startled half-breed with stunning force. Ginn, still wearing his Apache clothing, went down as the dark, powerful body of Jock Leclerc smothered him in a cursing, raging mesh of huge, flailing, slashing fists. Ginn half rose to one knee as Leclerc's knife went in under his upthrust arms and sank to the hilt in his chest. Ginn jumped up and ran like a rabbit for about twenty feet, then collapsed in a sodden heap. Leclerc walked over to him, pulled out his knife, looked apprehensively around, knelt self-consciously.

Caleb coughed and Leclerc jumped up and whirled, his face red and angry. "Ought to be ashamed o' yourself, scalpin' a poor dead renegade."

Leclerc's dark face lightened up, but the embarrassment remained. He poked the inert body with a blunt-toed boot. "I allow I oughta be, all right, but, dammit, I just couldn't resist it. Sort o' forgot I'm a civilized man fer a second there."

He forced a guilty smile, then frowned as he helped Caleb to his one good leg. "Wait a minute, *hombre.* Wa'n't that a hostile hair lock I seen, nice an' fresh, on your horse's bridle when we rode up here?"

Doorn's eyes were twinkling in spite of the bone weariness that was sapping his strength. "Well, that's different. I'm an outcast, an' folks sort o' expect that from me. But you. . . ."

Leclerc's powerful shoulders and arms half carried, half led Caleb back to the desolation of the Apache *ranchería*, where a group of perspiring soldiers were displaying trophies taken from those they had chased southward. "Ain't a man livin' that'll ever say anythin' about Caleb Doorn bein' a outcast in my presence." The soldiers looked up quickly from where they stood beside their horses, amid the settlers. Several officers looked a little embarrassed at Leclerc's words, and avoided Doorn's eyes.

Leclerc bristled as he helped Caleb astride his horse and clambered up on his own mount. His words were repeated in a truculent, loud voice. "Ain't a man livin' that'll speak evil o' Caleb·Doorn in my presence!" Leclerc's black eyes were wide and challenging and his massive shoulders were hunched as he stared at the silent officers.

An enlisted trooper, sweat-streaked and grinning slightly lopsidedly, nodded slowly. "No, I don't reckon they will. In your presence or out of it."

Jock tossed a sardonic look at the officers. "Now that you *hombres* finally got outen your little block-house, chase them hostiles y'selves. We're a-goin' back to Denton." He shook out his reins and moved off beside Caleb, whose thoughtful, brooding face wore a white, drawn, half smile.

As the settlers moved down the trail, one of the officers, a tall graying man standing stiffly among his subordinates, snapped a quick salute at the retreating back of the buckskin-clad ex-soldier riding beside Jock Leclerc, turned quickly, antagonistically, and frowned at the younger men. "There goes one of the men who'll make this land a safe place to live in."

The younger officers nodded slowly and wiped the beaded sweat from their faces.

Texas Herds
Bring Death

I

There was sultriness to the hot desert air that made even the lizards slow and lethargic, and Caleb Doorn looked up at the sullen sky. His gaze wandered over the trackless heaven and the brassy, blast-furnace lining was covered over with a dull gray opaqueness. He looked down over the tremendous sweep of the ageless land and let his eyes stop on a distant dust cloud that wound its way down out of the far mountains. A Texas herd. His gray, deep-set eyes were thoughtful and pensive. Since the end of the war, great Texas herds had been coming up into the northern territories. Texas was making a gallant effort to recover her shattered economy under the Confederacy and the Texas cattle were the medium. The big black gelding saw the dust and pointed his small, delicate ears. Caleb reached forward and patted his damp neck. The heat was intense as he reined around off the slight eminence, and started to ride down the narrow deer trail that led toward the little frontier town of Lodgepole.

Caleb Doorn was an average-size man dressed in the garb of a scout. His buckskin clothing was fringed, and the fringes swayed sinuously with the movement of his body as he rode into Lodgepole. The hostler at the livery barn nodded respectfully.

Caleb Doorn was a well-known man on the changing frontier. His exploits among the Indians were almost legends. To the red men, he was known as the Silent Outcast, a former cavalryman who spoke only when there was something worth saying.

After leaving his horse at the public barn, he strolled along Lodgepole's single, dust-coated road, past the raw, new buildings with their brave false fronts, and entered the only two-storied establishment in town, the Lincoln House Hotel. In the roughly furnished parlor, he saw the man he was looking for, Jack Britt, grizzled cowman whose ranches on the Verde made him one of the big men of the Lodgepole country.

"Texas herd comin', Jack. Crossin' the Big Sink right now, comin' from the direction of Taos."

Britt's close-cropped, gray head nodded thoughtfully. "I figgered there'd be one along afore too long." He looked up at Caleb. "Well, it'll mean trouble. The Crows won't let 'em go on upcountry with their herd, an' the local ranchers will fight 'em if they try to hold their herd on Lodgepole range. Barely enough grass fer local cows, let alone havin' enough to spare for an outside herd." Caleb was turning away. "Where ya goin'?"

"Over to see Bull Bear. See if I can't talk him into lettin' the Texans go on through."

"He won't let 'em."

"Maybe not, but if he would, it'd save some trouble. Anyway, maybe the Texans'll cut out a few stragglers an' give 'em to the Indians for a tribute. That used to work pretty well."

Britt shook his head dourly. "Won't work no more, Caleb. Them Crows rustle whatever they need nowadays." He shrugged resignedly. "Well, go to it. If anyone can talk sense into that redskin, you can. I'll hang around town until you get back. Maybe the Texans'll bivouac out in the sink before you get back, an' there won't be no trouble for anyone."

Caleb picked up his black horse at the livery barn and headed out onto the great prairie that began abruptly at the north end of Lodgepole. He rode with the grace of a born horseman. There had been no rain for two months and the feed was fast turning brown.

It took three hours of slow going to get to Bull Bear's camp. Wraith-like riders fell in behind him. He affected not to notice them following him in the shimmering distance. Crow scouts, he knew, had been posted strategically across the prairie to keep a close watch on Lodgepole. Caleb understood the Indian viewpoint easily enough. With no rain and the feed drying up, there was barely enough feed to keep the natural game from moving farther north. When the game left, the Indians would have to go, too. This, naturally, they didn't want to do; consequently they had drawn an imaginary deadline beyond which none of the white man's cattle could go.

Caleb rode past two sullen sentries, signaled that he came in peace, and was allowed to pass. The camp of Bull Bear was in a magnificent meadow fringed with a sprinkling of majestic pines that lent a delicate aroma to the grasslands where the conical, gaudily decorated teepees were scattered. Bull Bear's camp was in the hereditary upland of his people. From its slight eminence, the Indians could see the prairie around them for hundreds of miles. They could see the great dust clouds caused by the humpbacks, hours, sometimes days, before the buffalo would be close enough to kill. It was a favorite camp-

ing grounds of the Crows and in the rank, coarse
grass at their feet and the top two layers of mulch
could be found the discarded artifacts of their ances-
tors, indicating how ancient was the camp site.

Bull Bear's teepee was somewhat larger than the
others, being, in fact, a combination home and council lodge. Impressive symbols of the Crow tribe and
Bull Bear's fighting and hunting prowess were
daubed with Neolithic candor over the high structure. Four horses were tied to a crude hitch rail in
front of the teepee and a heraldic coup stick was
planted firmly in the ground in front, and a little to
one side, of the teepee opening. Caleb dismounted
under the curious glances of the Indians, who knew
him by sight, and entered the Great Plains home of
the Crow chieftain.

Inside, a caressing coolness swept over Caleb. He
stood respectfully just inside the flap, accustoming
his eyes to the shadowy gloom. A resonant voice
boomed out at him in English. "Silent Outcast, I have
been expecting you. Sit."

Caleb, who had a genuine affection for the scarred,
dusky man before him whose piercingly fierce eyes
were also genial and friendly, sat. Another man was
sitting beside Bull Bear. He was younger, with twin
streaks of red paint daubed horizontally across each
cheek, stretching from his nose to the area just below
each ear. He nodded with slight reserve and Caleb
nodded back. "Bull Bear, I am always glad to find my
welcome in the teepee of my brother. Why were you
expecting me?"

Bull Bear snorted. "Because my scouts told me
early this morning that a Texas herd was riding into
the Big Sink."

Caleb was mildly surprised. If the Crows knew

the herd was coming, they must have scouts completely around Lodgepole and far out on the plains south of town. "Why would I come to you because of a Texas herd?"

Bull Bear's face was touched by a faint smile. "Because you would want to get my permission to let the Texans cross Crow land. It is simple, Silent Outcast. Unless the Texans cross Crow land, there will be a fight with the Lodgepole cowmen. You would try to avert this."

Caleb looked for a long silent moment at the Indian. He had encountered perspicacity before, but never, that he could recall, had he run into an Indian who thought through to the end of a situation. Curious to see how far Bull Bear's reasoning had gone, he spoke again. "You are a wise man. What, then, is in the end?"

Bull Bear leaned forward a little. "There will be a fight among the white cowmen. Some will be killed. Some will give up and go back beyond the mountains. Others will hunt new ranges and new ways of driving their cows into the north country." He straightened up and smiled slightly. "The white men, who will stay in the land, are my brothers."

Caleb nodded solemnly. "This will happen unless you allow the Texans to cross Crow land."

"They cannot cross."

"Many men will die. . . ."

"White men, not red men."

"I see. You want the white men to fight among themselves. Even this small war might take some of the growing pressure of the whites off the Crows."

"Yes, Silent Outcast. The Indian has little left, but what he has, he must plan to keep." The powerful shoulders rose and fell eloquently and Caleb grudgingly admitted that, in reversed places, he, too, would act the same way. "Without our hunting lands and our hereditary homes, we are a lost people."

Doorn nodded sadly. "This is so." He arose slowly and the two Indians looked at him in impassive silence. "I am sorry."

As he turned to leave, Bull Bear spoke softly. "Silent Outcast, you are the Indian's brother. You, alone of your race, understand their side. May your God protect you in trouble ahead." Caleb nodded in salute, and left the teepee. As the gentle sound of his horse's shod hoofs sent back a retreating dull echo, Bull Bear turned to the younger man at his side. "In these troubled times, the Crows must stay out of trouble. When the white skins fight, they are like blind snakes. They strike out at anything. See that the fighting clans are told of this." He looked broodingly out the teepee flap where Caleb had so recently left. "Remember Silent Outcast well, Running Horse. He is the true friend of the Indian and a great fighting man. His coups are many and his gun never misses. He is your white brother."

II

When Caleb rode back into Lodgepole, dusk was falling. There was a small knot of loafers hanging around the livery barn when he put up his horse. When he walked past them on his way to the Lincoln House, he heard a snatch of conversation: "Well, they can't stop here. The boys are organizin' to run 'em off."

Caleb's face was bitter when he strode into the hotel. Jack Britt motioned him to a chair beside him, looked inquiringly into Caleb's face, and read his answer. He shook his head gravely. "You don't have to tell me. I can see it on your face."

"I don't blame the Indians, in a way."

Britt's blunt jaw locked irritably. "To hell with 'em. It wouldn't hurt nothin' if them cattle went through their lousy huntin' ground." He shrugged. "But if they say no, then that's it, I reckon."

Doorn could sense the tension in the air. "Anythin' interestin' happen while I was up at the Indian camp?"

Britt swore irritably in a low voice. "A little flurry o' excitement. Some o' the boys heard about the Texas herd an' come a-roarin' into town spittin' fire and damnation. I collared 'em an' told 'em to sit it

out an' we'd see what happens next. No sense
bustin' into trouble when it's comin' anyway."

"That all?"

"Not quite. The Texas critters are bedded down on
this side o' the sink. Feller name o' Chandler, big
raw-boned, rawhide sort o' fellow, is their trail boss.
He rode into town this afternoon an' the boys sent
him to me. I told him the situation an' he sort o'
laughed."

"What'd he say?"

" 'Bout what I figgered he'd say," Britt answered.
"He didn't have enough men to fight the whole
damned Crow nation, but that he had more'n enough
for me to see that his cows weren't run off the range
by a bunch of local cowboys. An' if he couldn't go
through the Crow land until he had worked up a big
bribe for 'em, he'd have to feed his critters offen our
feed. Said he was sorry as hell about it, but that's the
way it was."

Caleb got up and stretched. It had been a long day
for him. "I'm goin' to get some sleep. Tonight'll probably be about the best for sleepin' for the next few
days."

Brit nodded wryly. "You're more'n likely right at
that, Caleb. Well, I'm goin' back out to the ranch tonight, but I'll be back in Lodgepole by the time you've
eaten breakfast. Don't want to miss nothin', y'know."

Caleb ate at Sally Tate's café. It was a very frugal
place with hard puncheon benches along a low
counter of new fir. Sally was the orphaned daughter
of some emigrants that didn't make it. She was a
honey blonde with level, violet blue eyes, a luscious
full mouth, and a figure that made all the Lodgepole
cowboys sigh. Her nose wrinkled across the tiny
saddle of freckles when she saw Caleb enter.

He smiled back. "Sally, you're the prettiest woman in this café, y'know it?"

Her laugh was disturbing in a throaty way. "An' you're the prettiest man. Chili beans?"

"I reckon."

Caleb ate slowly and Sally leaned over the counter. "Caleb, is there something wrong in Lodgepole?"

"Why do you ask?"

"Every cowboy who's been in here today acts like he's afraid to kid me."

Caleb's deep eyes squinted in amusement. "Well, I'd say that was the best sign in the world. There's a Texas herd camped on this side of the sink."

"Oh." It sounded very small and the large violet eyes were on him with an unusual gravity. "Are you mixed up in it?"

"Uh, well, not exactly. I'm not a cattleman. I'm an old friend of Jack Britt's though. He and I used to scout for the Army together."

Sally's taffy hair waved when she nodded. "If Jack gets into it, you will, too, because he's your *compadre*, is that it?"

"Well, sort of. Y'see. . . ."

Sally straightened with an exasperated look on her face. "You men! You're like little children. This is no concern of yours, Caleb Doorn. Besides, if there's trouble, you might get hurt." Sally caught herself and blushed wildly.

Caleb looked up, a spoonful of chili beans poised in his hand. At that precise moment, the door slammed gently and Sally's flustered face raised and her eyes went quickly over the tall, recklessly smiling two-gun man who was drinking in her freshness with languid, bold eyes. The newcomer frowned a little and his small, dark eyes read Sally's embarrassment and his gaze dropped abruptly to Caleb's broad back. "This here squawman botherin' you, ma'am?"

Caleb felt the sting of the insinuation. Many new-comers to the northern country thought every white man who wore fringed buckskin was a squawman. Most, however, were very careful with the term. Graveyards all over the West were populated by men who had insulted others by calling them squawmen. The stranger saw the horror in Sally's eyes and didn't wait for her answer. With two large steps, he was beside Caleb and a talon-like hand grabbed for the scout's shoulder. "In Texas, we don't tolerate no insultin' o' women, squawman!"

Caleb was out from under the reaching fingers of steel, on his feet, facing the man. Texan was stamped all over him. He was obviously one of the drovers with the Texas herd. Caleb noted the two tied-down guns, too. Texas gunfighter. He shook his head slowly and his eyes were frosty. "This young lady happens to be a friend of mine, an', if I were you, Texan, I'd go easy on that squawman term up here."

There was a sneer on the tall man's face. "Y'would, would ya? Well down in Texas. . . ."

"You're not down in Texas now."

The man's face darkened. He looked contemptuously at the smaller man for a second, then one long, wiry fist shot out. Caleb rolled with it and the blow glanced off his shoulder. The Texan was making a very common and fatal error. He was over confidently underestimating the man in front of him. Caleb had fought the best brawlers on the frontier, Indian and white, and he was respected by both. He moved forward on the balls of his feet with the speed of light, and a massively muscled arm shot out. The Texan looked surprised when it smashed into his stomach. He went over a little to take some of the shock out of the blow.

Sally Tate, ashen-faced and horrified, was rigid behind the counter as the tall Texan swore violently and lunged at Caleb. The scout wasn't there when the stranger's ham-like fist, a bludgeon of bone and sinew, whipped into the hot atmosphere. Caleb stepped clear of the furiously charging gunman, ducked under the long arms, and bore in. He shot a rock-like fist into the Texan's stomach that stopped the larger man. Before the gunman could recover, another bone and muscle piston crashed into his chest, and the third, as the Texan was rocking back on his high boot heels, slammed into his jaw like the kick of a mule. There was a loud popping sound, sharp and clear in the charged atmosphere, and the Texan went down half in, half out of the café, his head and shoulders lying through the half-opened door.

Caleb turned and looked at Sally. Her large eyes were glassy. "Sit down, Sally. Get a hold of yourself. I'm awfully sorry. It shouldn't have happened in here."

A rush of color came back into the girl's cheeks as she turned to Caleb. "Is he dead?" Caleb looked down at the stunned Texan and shook his head. Sally let a long, pent-up gust of air out of her lungs. "Caleb Doorn"—the violet eyes were snapping angrily with released tension and relief—"you've hurt that man badly. You ought to be ashamed, Caleb. You had no right. . . ."

Caleb was halfway up the plank sidewalk toward his room at the Lincoln House, before the voice finally died away behind him. He was amused at Sally's reaction and irritated at the overbearing arrogance of the Texan, and, when his mind reviewed the happenings of the day, he felt foreboding over what the future held. If all the drovers with the Texas herd were of the same stripe, there would be no way to avoid trouble. The hotel was dark when Caleb went up to his room. The bed felt good, and, until he sank down into it with a comfortable sigh, he had had no idea how tired he was.

When Caleb awoke, it was to find a pair of worried, squinted blue eyes, faded and anxious, bending over him. "Come on. Hell, ya can't sleep all day."

"No? Jack, you don't know me, once I'm in one of these manmade beds." He swung his feet out of the bed and reached for his boots and britches with a prodigious yawn. "You get run off the ranch this morning? Hell, it's twenty miles from your place on the Verde to Lodgepole. You must've gotten astride before sunup."

Britt rolled a lumpy cigarette while he waited for Caleb to finish his toilet. His voice drowned out the splashing of the scout at the commode set on the marble-topped dresser. "Well, dammit all, I didn't allow I'd have to come to town till later, but some of the Box J boys come by last night, pretty late, an' tol' me that some firebrand laid out the foreman of the Texans in Sally Tate's café." He popped the cigarette into his mouth having lit it with an angry gesture. Through a cloud of grayish smoke, his voice was edgy and harsh. "As if trouble ain't comin' fast enough, some damned fool has to beat hell outen the ramrod of that trail herd, makin' trouble a certainty now. Oh, Lord, sometimes I wished I'd never seen this burned-out corner of hell."

Caleb cocked his head a little as he held up the worn towel to dry his face. "Ain't that rain, Jack?"

"Sure it's rain. Been rainin' off an' on all night. Well"—the hard lines softened a little—"that's one blessing, anyway. Now the grass'll come back."

Doorn rubbed himself musingly. "Jack, that Texas gunman came into Sally's lookin' for trouble. I'm the one that downed him."

Britt looked up incredulously. "You?"

"Yep. He didn't leave me any choice."

Britt groaned and took a deep draw on the quirly in his hand. "Well, I know you ain't a troublemaker, so he more'n likely got just what he was after. But it sure clinches things."

"I'm sorry, Jack."

"Did you say he was a gunman?"

"I reckon. Anyway, he had two tied-down guns an' that look about him, if you know what I mean."

Britt nodded curtly. "I know what you mean, all right. Well, let's go down an' get some breakfast."

Sally glared at Caleb when she set the thick plates of fried eggs and side meat down in front of them. "Bad enough to knock him unconscious, but why did you have to leave him here for me to take care of?"

Caleb shrugged and smiled. "The way you were eatin' into me, I figured I'd be safer with a nest of mountain lions, so I left. Did he say much after he come around?"

Sally smiled lopsidedly. "Well, nothing complimentary, I can assure you. He wanted to know who you were and I told him. Also, he said he'd be back today with his crew and they were going to take over Lodgepole, as well as all the grass land they needed to run their cattle on, until their boss figured out what they were going to do about the Crows' refusal to let them go on north."

Jack Britt finished his breakfast, paid Sally, and got up. "Sally, I wish you'd get married."

The girl was startled and looked up quickly. "Why, Jack?"

"Because you're the only one I've every known who could make this *hombre* settle down." He wagged his head solemnly at the red-faced girl and ignored Doorn's embarrassed frown. "He'll never amount to a damn, Sally, till you take him in hand. The West is changin', girl. Scouts an' the like are a lost breed now. It's goin' to be a cowman's West, an', if you'll get him shook outen those fringed suits, he'll make his pile along with the rest o' us."

Caleb was smiling dourly at his old friend. He nodded at Sally with a wink. "Sure must be somethin' in what he says, Sally. That's the longest speech I ever heard him make. Scouts turned cowmen sure get windy, don't they?"

Jack growled under his breath. "Come on, Caleb. Let's go see this here imported town marshal Lodgepole hired a few months back. They tell me he's a ripsnorter from down in New Mexico Territory."

III

Marshal Holt was a hard-eyed, lean-jawed man of middle age with a bear trap line for a mouth and an angular, spare body to match. Only his thinning gray hair gave a clue to his age, and that seldom was uncovered from beneath the low-crowned, flat-brimmed hat he wore tilted slightly forward, low over his slate gray eyes. "Yeah, Britt, I heard it was comin'." The bony shoulders rose and fell. "Well, let 'er come. I'll kill the first gunman who draws a gun in Lodgepole. That's my job."

Caleb studied the marshal and didn't particularly care for what he saw. Marshal Holt was a killer, through and through. Cold, unemotional, and ruthless. Jack Britt frowned heavily. "Oh, I don't think we gotta take any such quick action as that. Do. . . ."

"Look, Britt. This here is my headache, not yours. I get paid to keep the peace, and, by Gawd, I'll keep 'er. Any o' them Texans come into town huntin' trouble, I'll handle 'em."

Without a word, Caleb and Jack left Marshal Holt's office. On the plank sidewalk outside, Jack's smoky eyes were narrowed a little. He pulled his coat a little closer about him. The rain was starting again and its tiny fingers were cool on the back of

his neck. "I'll be damned if I like what's comin',
Caleb. That marshal's a gun hawk if I ever saw one.
Oh, hell"—he turned up the walk toward the Long-
horn Saloon—"let's go get a drink."

Caleb pulled the flat, stiff brim of his low-
crowned hat down over his eyes. The rain didn't
bother him half as much as the brusque town marshal did. They walked among the huddled people
on the sidewalk and edged into the saloon. A
rancher was loudly praising the rain over a tin cup
of lukewarm beer. He raised the cup with one hand,
his luxurious mustache with the other, and drank
with loud, gurgling sounds. There were about fifteen Lodgepole townsmen and cattlemen in the
place. A sprinkling of younger cowboys, flushed
and alert, were scattered through the crowd. In a far
corner, a poker game was going full tilt, the players
impassively smoking and ignoring the rest of the
room.

"What'll it be, gents?"

"Couple o' beers, Sam."

The tin cups slid before Caleb and Jack, and the
bartender looked at them anxiously. "Trouble's
brewin', boys."

Jack drank a little and nodded sourly. "You ain't
tellin' us nothing, Sam."

"No? Well, there was three o' them Texans in here
a while back, an' one of 'em was a big *hombre* with
tied-down guns. They didn't stay long, just looked
us over an' left."

Caleb was surprised that they were in town so
early. He said nothing and drank his beer slowly,
eyes on the backbar mirror. Jack Britt shrugged.
"Most o' the cowmen been in, Sam?"

The bartender nodded wryly. "Hell, yes. I reckon

every cowman fer a hundred miles been here once or twice this mornin'." He shook his head. "They're wanderin' aroun' town like lost dogs, lookin' to be in the right place at the right time, I reckon."

"You there, at the bar. Squawman!"

The room got suddenly quiet enough to hear men breathing. Caleb had seen them come in while the bartender and Jack had been talking. He had seen the lanky foreman of the Texans single him out to the crowd of cold-eyed, bronzed-faced men behind him. Caleb set the beer cup down easily and answered without turning around. "If you mean me, *Tejano*, remember what I told you about callin' folks squawman up in this country."

The big man's hands were poised to swoop for his tied-down guns and his even, white teeth were visible through the flat lips. "Turn aroun', squawman!"

Caleb didn't move. He calmly studied the hard faces behind the foreman. "How many men you got there, *gringo salido?*"

The insult was worse than being called a squawman, and the Texans all knew it. The foreman ripped out an obscene oath. "Enough to take care of any Lodgepole cowmen who want to buy into this game."

"Well, Texan, tell 'em to get out from behind you, 'cause these boys aren't doin' my fightin' for me an' I don't want to hit some man I don't have nothin' against."

The Texan crouched a little lower. His voice was soft and deep. "All right, squawman, it's just between us, then. Turn around an' take your medicine."

Out of all the witnesses to that fight, none could ever swear that they saw what happened. There was a blur of action, a swish of fringes, and the Long-horn Saloon was rocked by two deafening explosions that were magnified by the four walls and roof. There were no second shots. This was a gun-fight between two thoroughly experienced gunmen. One shot each; that is all it took. For a long moment, there was a deathly silence, then the bartender spoke up in a rasping, small voice: "See if he's dead, boys."

None of the local men went forward and two of the Texans, hesitatingly, looking uneasily at the Lodgepole cowmen and the cowboys, walked gin-gerly over and bent over their foreman's sprawled, still form. One of the riders looked up at Caleb, still standing against the bar, his voice small with awe. "Plumb through the head." There was a rash of movement at the batwing doors and Marshal Holt, savage eyes slitted in his hawk-nosed face, hat brim low and menacing, stood just inside the opening. "Who done it?"

Caleb nodded. "I did."

"Witnesses?"

Holt's hard, flat voice broke the spell and the room buzzed as some men turned to the marshal while others turned to their neighbors and began talking in strained voices. Holt came over beside Doorn. "Must've been self-defense, from what ever'body says." He let his cold eyes travel the full length of the scout and back. "I knew that *hombre*, once. He was Powder Hudson, one of the killingest gunmen in the Southwest." Marshal Holt shook his head slightly. "Don't see how ya done it. There's goin' to be trouble here, *hombre*, an' I don't want you in town when it hits. Git your horse an' slope."

Caleb's thoughtful gaze was direct and calm. "You've made a mistake, Marshal. That man asked for what he got, an' I'm not leavin' Lodgepole because I defended myself."

Holt's eyes blazed suddenly with a crazy light. "I say you are, *hombre*."

Jack Britt stepped up, red-faced. "Holt, you're the marshal here, not the governor. You don't order any respectable citizen outen Lodgepole, now or any other time."

For a second, Holt's body tensed and his face went white. Caleb was watching for the little telltale tightening around the edges of the mouth. Several of the other Lodgepole men came forward. Three of them were prominent cowmen.

"Jack's right, Marshal. This here man's got as much right here in Lodgepole as you have. He stays."

Holt looked at the tight knot of angry cowboys and ranchers around him, estimated his chances at nil, and relaxed with a savage smile. "Can't argue with the whole damned town." He swung back to Doorn. "What I said still goes, *hombre*. You got till midnight tonight."

Doorn smiled softly. "That's all the time I'll need, Marshal."

Marshal Holt held the door open for two of the Texans who struggled through with the remains of Powder Hudson, ramrod of the Texas trail herd. Several of the Texans tossed hard looks at the Lodgepole cowmen as they went out. Jack Britt tossed off the rest of his beer with a big sigh. "Well, boys, unless I've got these Texans sized up all wrong, hell's goin' to pop loose any minute now."

The old white-headed man, who had argued with Holt over Doorn's leaving town, shrugged. "I wouldn't bet on it, Jack. Them coyotes are pretty much all air, and now, with their foreman shot down, they just might take their damned critters an' head out around the Lodgepole country an' go on up north by way of Cañon del Muerto."

Jack was looking thoughtfully at the older man when the bartender spoke up. "Here, you fellers, have a beer on the house. Gawd that was the quickest gunfight I ever seen. Two shots an' it's over. Did'ja see where that Texan's shot went?"

Caleb shook his head dryly. "No. As long as it didn't go through me, I don't care."

"Right here. Look. Man that was awful close." Caleb and the others looked down at the front of the bar. The dead man's slug had missed Caleb's body by a fraction of an inch and had gone through the bar front and out through the back wall. "Close, damned awful close, I'd call it."

"Where ya goin', Caleb?" Britt's grizzled eyebrows were creased with a worried look.

"Down to the livery barn an' check on my horse. Back in a few minutes."

As Caleb emerged from the saloon, the people on the plank sidewalk looked at him oddly, and the buzz of excited voices trailed in his wake from the saloon all the way down to the livery barn. The half-breed hostler flashed a brilliant smile at him as he walked back and looked in at his drowsing black horse, sleek and shiny and comfortable, a big flake of fragrant timothy hay still untouched in the worn manger.

"Good fight. I heard about it."

Caleb was mildly irritated that the news had traveled so quickly. He nodded and ignored the quick look of anticipation. "Saddle my horse and hang the bridle on the saddle horn. Tie him in his stall. I may have to use him in a hurry. Understand?"

The half-breed nodded importantly. He now had a secret that the other loungers would know nothing about.

Caleb turned and walked out of the wide opening of the barn. Somewhere a rifle cracked and Caleb heard the ripping tear of the heavy slug as it plowed its way into the wall beside him. He threw himself backward, ran into the barn again, down the long, dirt-paved aisle between the stalls, past the startled hostler, and out the back end. It was beginning to rain again and a freshet of cool, invigorating air blew into his face, fragrant with the smell of wet, moldy earth and sage.

Caleb's fringed hunting shirt darkened as the rain fell on it. He stalked slowly, warily around in back of the stores and avoided the rubbish and refuse piles, alive with shiny bluebottle flies, with effortless grace. The Texans were back for blood. He was opposite the Longhorn Saloon when the throbbing rumble of loping horses came to his ears. He stepped around in front of the building he had been using as a screen as a large host of heavily armed men swung up to the hitch rail and dismounted. Two tight-faced men were left to watch the horses and the rest of the riders surged into the saloon. Caleb stepped out into plain sight and both the Texans left with the horses saw him at the same time. One made a slight, bird-like jerk toward his gun and growled. The second man said something in a breathless voice and the first man stopped his dip. Caleb held them both with his cold stare and neither man moved. The speed of the scout's draw had made a deep impression on the Texan who had been present at the recent killing, and he had stopped the green cowboy just in time.

IV

All of Lodgepole, it seemed, had expected the Texans to return. There was only the gentle whisper of the light drizzle to break the awful silence in the town. Even as far away as Caleb was, he could hear the stentorian roar of a big, deep-chested man in the saloon.

"Ah want the squawman who done shot mah fo'-man an', b' Gawd, iffen y'all don't produce him right naow, I'll tear this heah li'l dung heap daown aroun' yuah ears."

There was the brittle silence again, then Caleb heard the scuffling boots and tinkling spurs as the Texans came through the batwing doors. They were beside their horses before the horse guard pointed at him and yelled in a high, hysterical voice: "Thar he stan's! Over thar ag'in' that store. He's the feller as shot down Powder Hudson."

The Texans all went into action at the same time. It was a fair certainty that they were letting off pent-up steam, because at least a dozen of them couldn't have seen the horse guard point to him. Caleb singled out a massive, flashily dressed man with an explosive, blustering face. His gun was clear of its holster before the horse guard had stopped speaking. The big man swore thunderously and filled his hand. Caleb's shot sent the big pistol flashing backward out of his hand, then Caleb disappeared down the slim alley between the two buildings. The Texan roared in rage and pain and leaped on his horse. "Comb th' town. Teah th' damned thang daown, but get me thet squawman. Ah'll give a hunnert dollars gold to th' cowboy that brings me that *hombre* daid or alive."

Marshal Holt had heard the firing and was just emerging from his office when a covey of the red-eyed cowboys swung past. One of them turned sideways in the saddle and fired a careless shot at the marshal. With one smooth motion, the marshal's gun was flaming. The rider went off over backward and his frightened horse ran after the others, stirrups flapping and head high.

All hell broke loose. Lodgepole seemed finally to let go its pent-up emotion. Rifles cracked and pistols roared. The Texans, embattled and savage, shot indiscriminately at anything that moved. Two stray dogs and one saddle horse lay where they had been cut down in the deserted street, not far from the cowboy who had been shot off his horse by Marshal Holt. From the Longhorn Saloon, spiteful pistol fire erupted. The Lodgepole cowmen sought targets with little chance of success. The fight had swirled almost out of range. With a sizzling oath, one of the younger Lodgepole riders darted through the batwing doors while the others watched. They all wanted to get outside, but feared the consequences of leaving as long as the Texans were loose on the town. The rider ran about fifty feet, when a ragged volley of rifle fire rattled up and down the road. He crumpled in a heap, and the drizzling rain diluted the little pools of blood that formed around his dead body.

Britt wagged his head. "Not that way, boys. It's murder goin' out the front. See if they ain't a back way."

There was, the bartender showed it to them, and singly and in pairs the Lodgepole men got away from the besieged saloon. With the scattered defenders slipping through town, the fight became general. Marshal Holt was very effectively bottled up in his office, however, and his furious oaths rang over the intermittent gunfire. Storming and fuming, the fighting lawman challenged one and all of the malcontents to fight him. All he got in the way of replies was a bouquet of bullets that kept him indoors.

Caleb had scaled the back wall of the general store. He could hear the spurs of the running Texans below him. In the smattering of gunfire, he heard one Texan swear plainly and another laugh. Squirming along, prone, Caleb risked a peek over the edge of the building. One Texan was exploring his rump, which had been grazed by a rifle slug. He had holstered his gun and was alternating between swearing with feeling and groaning. The second cowboy was hunkered low behind a half-filled water barrel. Even as Caleb watched, the man levered his rifle and pumped a shot into the window of Sally Tate's café.

Caleb eased his .44 over the edge of the roof and spoke: "You, there, pull up your britches an' help your pardner climb up here."

To say the Texans were startled would be putting it incorrectly. They were dumbfounded. Awkwardly they clambered up to Caleb, who kept them covered. Once on the roof, he ordered them both to lie down, then disarmed and tied them with their own belts. Gags were made from their neckerchiefs and handkerchiefs, and the frontiersman smiled saturninely at them as he dropped off the roof.

Caleb was taking advantage of every foot of cover among the refuse piles and out buildings on his way to the livery stable. The rain was coming down now in a heavy drizzle that was cold in contrast to the former heat. The gun butt was slippery in his hand. Up ahead, two men were backing around the end of a building, and the scout hastily ducked into an outhouse until he saw whether they were Lodgepole men or Texans. Unfortunately for Caleb, the outhouse turned out to be occupied by another hiding fighter. With an alarmed oath, the man fired his gun as Caleb spun away as far as the tight confines of the building would allow. The bullet scored a thin, hot scratch under Doorn's ribs. He felt it as he fired back and the tiny shack rocked on its hollowed-out foundations. The door fell on its hinges as Caleb's body went against it and he fell outside in the slippery mud. The two men farther down turned white-faced at the eruption of the two shots. With an oath, one of them fired and missed. The word—"Squawman!"— split the air and Doorn rolled as fast as he could in the muck, finally getting to one knee.

The Texans were the brace of horse guards he had seen in front of the saloon. The older one was firing with frantic haste and no attempt at accuracy. Caleb ran as he crouched, his gun spitting fire. The older man went down, and the younger jumped and fled. A rifle crashed behind him and Caleb went down into the mud as he whirled. Standing, spraddle-legged, a Winchester carbine held waist high in both hands, the big, florid-looking Texan levered and fired again. Caleb threw two quick shots at the man, jumped to his feet, and ran zigzag for the dark interior of the livery barn. It was shadowy and dark inside, but the sour smell of powder smoke rode the atmosphere like a warning.

Jack Britt could hear Marshal Holt cursing in an embittered monologue and a little wry smile tugged at the corners of his mouth. Nothing could be quite so annoying to one of the marshal's fire-eating propensities as to be bottled up inside his own office when a gunfight was going on in town. He hugged the wall of the Lincoln House closer as a rifle flamed off toward the livery stable. There were two muffled pistol shots from behind the barn and down a little way, and Jack wondered who had gotten caught back there. He soon forgot, however, when a Lodgepole cowboy fell soddenly onto the overhang in front of the general store from the roof above. The body didn't roll and Jack's squinted eyes looked for the killer. A wisp of a black hat showed down the deserted street from him, on his side of the road. He cocked his pistol and waited. The black hat's curled edges came out a trifle, and Jack carefully brought his gun up. A rash of sudden firing in the neighborhood of the Longhorn drove the gunman back to cover again. Jack waited patiently until the hat came into view again. This time there was enough for a target. He fired methodically and the hat went sailing off into space like a frightened bird and its owner looked down the road at Jack for one startled second and disappeared. Jack moved, too.

Inside the livery stable, Caleb took a breather behind a jag of aromatic mountain hay. The cut along his ribs had bled profusely but the mud caking he had acquired while rolling around in the alley had pretty well staunched it. His fringed shirt was a wreck. Grimly he wiped his .44 off as best he could and reloaded it. Suddenly he heard a board creak lightly, too lightly to be moved by any of the softly snorting, excited horses in the stalls. He tensed unconsciously and let his eyes roam familiarly through the eerie gloom of the building. Again he heard it and flattened out on his stomach, poking his head around one ragged corner of the haystack. A big Texan was quietly stalking through the barn looking for him. Smiling bitterly, Caleb's pistol came up slowly, steadied, and fired with a thunderous explosion. The Texan's rifle went off unpredictably as Caleb's slug tore its stock into a gust of splinters. The big man staggered forward as the gun was wrenched out of his hands. He roared in pain and insane fury and hurled himself toward the haystack. Caleb cocked his gun again, but the big man, despite his bulk, was upon him before he could squeeze off the second shot, his ornate boot toe lashing out instinctively and sending Caleb's gun flying. The scout barely had time to get to his feet before the cowman was on him. A sizzling fist the size of a small ham roiled the air past Caleb's head and another gigantic hand slammed him backward, striking him fully in the chest. Caleb gasped and rolled away from the behemoth of ferocity that was boring in, roaring mad.

Caleb found an inner well of energy somewhere and came back on the balls of his feet. He recognized this fight as one for his life. The Texan was insanely angry and his tremendous body was capable of deadly force. He lashed out and the Texan took the blow without an effort to side-step. Caleb had struck hard, but the Texan smothered the shocking force as though he hadn't felt it. A little awe surged through the frontiersman as he back-pedaled. The stranger charged, head down, roaring oaths, his big arms flailing like a thresher. Again Caleb gave way, but this time he went a little sideways and chopped two stunning blows under the Texan's ear that staggered the big man. Following up what he thought was an advantage, Caleb drove in with a rain of piston-like shots that caromed off the hard body of the other man like rubber balls.

A big fist lashed out in a looping, overhand shot and Caleb went down. The Texan stood over him, legs apart, breathing heavily for a second. Caleb shot one boot toe behind the big man's calf and darted the other foot out like the tongue of a snake, pushing it abruptly against the Texan's kneecap. With a look of surprise, the big man went over backward, hard. Before he could regain his feet, Caleb was up and poised. When the Texan came up off the floor, a one-two lash out of bony, knuckled fists belted him like the explosions of a bullwhip in the face. He teetered for a long second and went down again, a bubbling, ragged sound of breathing coming out of his smashed nose.

Caleb felt weak as he scooped up his .44 and walked heavily toward the front of the barn. The firing was getting faster now and he edged carefully up to the yawning maw of the front entrance, risked a quick peek that drew no fire, drew in his breath, and made an erratic, reckless rush for the opposite side of the road. Dust devils kicked up mud behind him as the Texas cowboys swung to gun him down, but he made it to the back of the apothecary's shop with only one boot heel missing and two holes through the back of his tattered hunting shirt that he knew nothing about. Leaning against the soggy wood of the building, he caught his breath as his narrowed eyes studied the immediate locality without seeing a single fighter. Knowing the Texans on his side of the road would be moving in on him, he reluctantly pushed himself off the wall and began a weary advance down past the Longhorn Saloon to Sally Tate's café.

V

lmost before his slippery pistol butt rapped on the thick back door of Sally's café, the door opened and Caleb shoved through. Sally's violet eyes were wide in alarm. "Caleb, you're hurt!" She went forward, but he backed away with a tired shake of his head and a tight smile.

"No, just scratched. Are you all right?"

Sally's tension relaxed as it had the night before when Caleb had left the now defunct Texan on her floor, unconscious. Sparks flashed from the deep blue eyes and her lips trembled. "Look at you! You're mud from the top of your head to your boot toes. Don't stand there and drip that slime all over my clean floor . . . get over there by the stove." Caleb moved to obey and caught the flicker of a swift movement out of the corner of his eye. Instantly his muscles jerked into action as he whirled and his gun came out and up with incredible speed. Sally stood horrified, her mouth open and one hand at her chest.

"No shoot."

Caleb let the breath come out of him in a rasping sob. "That was close, Bull Bear. Damned close."

The Crow leader nodded wryly. "Too close. You hurt?"

"No, tired and filthy from wallowing in the mud

out there." Caleb nodded toward a rain-flecked window where the slippery, dark earth was shiny with water. "But not hurt."

"You stop fight, then."

"Huh?"

"You stop fight. Crows let Texas cows go to the Platte if cowmen let Crow warriors guide them through Crow land by way of Cañon del Muerto."

Caleb looked thoughtfully at the scarred warrior before he answered. Cañon del Muerto—Dead Man's Cañon—was aptly named. The trail was narrow above a deep cañon. Many emigrants had been ambushed there in the early days. Now, even with the Crows to guide them, the cañon trail would be a treacherous, slippery quagmire. Still, it was preferable to the fighting at that time still echoing through Lodgepole. Anything, Doorn thought, to get rid of the Texans and their cattle. He nodded abruptly. "I'll see what I can do." He turned and opened the door a crack before Sally Tate caught his slippery, mud-covered arm.

"Caleb, don't go. They'll kill you. Oh, Caleb. . . ."

"Sally, I've got to try an' stop the killing. Bull Bear's offer to cross. . . ."

"I don't care, Caleb. You're hurt. Stay here and let me bandage your side and wash the mud off you. Let someone else go."

Caleb fixed her with a critical look. "Who?"

She looked around her for a desperate moment, saw only the blank, disapproving look of the Crow chieftain, and let her arm drop as Caleb slipped out of the café into the drizzle and mud.

The rain was coming down in a steady, persistent sheet of water now and Doorn was thoroughly drenched and streaked with the cloying mud before he managed to get to the Longhorn. A bullet came out of nowhere, smashed into the rear door of the saloon, knocking it violently inwards. Caleb jumped frantically into the room, crouched and ready, but saw no one. He swung over to the stairway leading upstairs and mounted them two at a time, a filthy, grim figure of a man, hair straggling over his grimy, hollow-eyed face, the wet .44 glistening in his muddy paw.

Caleb searched each room until he found what he was looking for, a small trap door in the ceiling leading up onto the roof. With surprising ability, he leaped up, caught on with his powerful fingers, and shoved the wooden cover away so that he could wiggle through. The rain hit him like a hundred cold little fists as he clambered out onto the roof. Straightening up, he was startled to see a crouched rifleman over beside the edge of the building's false front. Apparently the drenching rain had muffled his noisy ascent. Stealing forward, he raised and cocked his six-gun. "Drop it *hombre*, or I'll drop you."

The lean back tensed but the rifle fell into the pool of clear water at the man's feet. Caleb risked a quick glance down over the town. He could command the front of the livery barn easily from up here and it dawned on him where the gunman had been who had first shot at him as he had emerged from the stable.

"Turn around, but don't raise up too high or you'll get it from down below." The man turned. Doorn recognized him as one of the men who had been with the gunman foreman at the saloon. The man's eyes widened when he saw the filthy, ragged apparition before him. He recognized Caleb as the killer of his foreman and a dry tongue flickered over his rain-washed face. "What's the name of that big *hombre*

with the flashy clothes? The one who did all the hol-
lerin' in the saloon this mornin'?"

"Jeff Chandler. He's the owner o' the cattle. He's a
big man down in. . . ."

"Who was the other feller? The one I killed?"

"Powder Hudson. He was the foreman o' Chandler's trail drives."

"What's your name?"

"Buck Gleason."

"Got a good pair of lungs, Buck?"

"I reckon, why?"

"Go over to the edge of the false front, where you
were, an' holler out for Chandler."

"Like hell," the answer came from a white and
frightened face. "You won't make no Judas outen me.
I ain't callin' Jeff out so's you can gun him down."

"I'm not going to shoot him, Buck. I want to
palaver about movin' the herd out o' here. The Crows
just gave permission to cross their land. Now holler
out!"

The cowboy stood undecidedly and Caleb's big
gun came up persuasively. The Texan licked his lips
again and turned away. He went to the edge of the
false front, cupped his hand over his mouth, and
yelled for Chandler. The gunfire dropped off as the
fighters down below looked for the man behind the
voice. Again Gleason yelled, and this time an answer came back. Gleason turned and looked hope-
fully at Caleb. "Now what?"

"Tell him to come out an' palaver."

It took a little yelling back and forth, but finally
Chandler came hesitatingly out of the livery barn
and the gunmen held their fire when Caleb yelled
for them to hold off. Pushing Gleason up beside him,
Caleb stepped into full view on the roof. He felt a

glow of satisfaction at the swollen, purplish, blood-splattered appearance of the massive cowman.

"Chandler, the Crows have just agreed to let your herd go on up north, providin' you'll agree to let 'em guide you the way they want you to go."

Chandler's baleful eyes recognized the dripping figure on the roof as the "squawman". His big fists opened and closed convulsively. For a long moment, he didn't reply. Then he shrugged slightly. He'd like nothing better than to fight the Lodgepole men until they were all dead, then fire their miserable little town, but right now the cattle were the important thing. He shrugged again grimly and his sullen eyes were vicious above the wreckage of his face. He'd come back another time and wipe this Yankee scum off the face of the earth. "All right. Put up your guns an' help us move our cattle out an' we'll go."

Lodgepole came back to stilted life. The wounded were cared for in the Longhorn Saloon where benches were collected hastily and assembled into hard beds. The dead were duly identified and turned over to their respective allies for burial. Jeff Chandler, indignant more than pained, stood bitterly in the middle of the room talking to Jack Britt and Caleb, writhing inwardly under the stares of his cowboys and the Lodgepole men alike, his clothing splattered with the blood from his broken nose and purplish eyes.

"Bull Bear is down in the café. He says you can cross the Crow country if you'll go by way of Cañon del Muerto, thus staying off the hunting grounds of his people. He also said that he'd let you pass only if you'll let Crow warriors act as guides," Caleb said.

"Where is this Injun?"

"I'll go get him." Caleb turned abruptly and left the

cluttered, uncomfortable atmosphere of the Longhorn, where both factions were eyeing each other sullenly and tending to the injured.

Jack Britt frowned as he surveyed the big man's
face. "Want some clean water an' salve fer your face?"

Chandler's brows contracted in a thunderous expression. "No, damn ya!"

Britt shrugged and moved away, leaving the Texan
alone in the noisy, tense room while he went among
the Lodgepole men. When Caleb returned with Bull
Bear, resplendent in a fiery red blanket and carrying
a brand new Henry repeating rifle, Britt drifted back
to the little group that had gathered around Chandler. The Texan glowered at the straight, square-
jawed Indian. "Who d'ya think ya are, redskin,
tellin' Texans where they can cross . . . ?"

"None o' that!" Everyone turned and looked at the
speaker. Marshal Holt, livid-faced and ramrod erect,
was standing in the doorway. "You got your terms,
Texan. Either take 'em or leave 'em!" There was no
mistaking the raging fury behind the words. Holt's
anger at being kept out of the fight showed on his face
and no one in the room doubted his eagerness or ability to go for the tied-down guns on his legs.

Chandler swapped hard stares with him, saw no
compromise in the rabid, faded eyes, and shrugged,
turning back to Bull Bear. "We'll be ready to drive
out with th' dawn. Have your men thar!"

VI

Caleb and Jack Britt sat beside the singing stove in the kitchen of Sally's café, drinking coffee. Bull Bear drank one cup and left after agreeing to have his warriors at the Texan's camp before sunup.

"Caleb, you look sort o' used up." Britt's critical eyes scanned the filthy, ragged scarecrow beside him. He turned to Sally. "Ain't you got a dry shirt an' maybe a pair o' britches aroun' here some place he could borrow?"

Sally shook her head as she poured the second cup of steaming coffee into the heavy white mugs. There was a mantle of dark red in her cheeks. "No. Of course not. This is a café, not a clothing store."

Caleb smiled lopsidedly. "I'll go down to the general store in a few minutes an' get something dry. Jack, ya reckon that Chandler *hombre*'s over his mad?"

Britt shook his head gravely. "No. Not by a damned sight. He's a hard man, Caleb. I've seen a lot just like him. They never give up."

"Reckon I'll sort o' go along with 'em on their drive then. Don't want 'em pickin' trouble with the Crows."

Britt set his empty coffee cup down and got up in his soggy clothes. "Well, that'd be a damned quick fight. Old Bull Bear's got about five to one with them

Texans." He shook his head again. "He may be a sorehead, but I don't think he's that mad. Well, I gotta get back to the ranch. If you ride over the cañon with 'em, Caleb, you probably won't be back till tomorrow night. I'll see you at the Lincoln House then." He opened the back door and stepped out into the rain with a wry shake of his head. "It'll take me till then to get wrung out." The door closed behind him, and Caleb looked over at Sally.

"Scared?" he asked.

"Of course. Caleb, you ask the silliest questions some times." She blushed at her own boldness and got off her chair briskly. "I'll go over to the emporium and get you some new clothes." He watched her walk out of the room with an amused smile on his face. It would be interesting to see what she brought back.

When Caleb finally returned to the cold room in the Lincoln House, his side ached. Not so much from the bullet groove under his ribs as from the laughter that had threatened to engulf him at Sally's indignation when he wouldn't wear the elegant, ankle-choker pants and shiny derby she had bought. He had left her as he had the night before, under the whiplash of her tongue, gone to the emporium himself, and purchased a new pair of California pants and a butternut shirt, then gone to his room and laughed himself to sleep.

Dawn was a pink wraith of cleanliness over the steaming, wet world when Caleb mounted his black gelding and rode south out of Lodgepole. The new clothes were a little stiff and he ruefully looked at them in the light of day and wished he had his old fringed shirt back. The mud was slippery and heavy on his horse's hoofs as he rode. He was almost within smelling distance of the Texas cow camp when he was joined by a Crow Indian who came silently out of the brush and reined in beside him. He recognized the youth as the painted warrior he had seen in Bull Bear's teepee two days before.

"I remember you, but don't know your name."

"Running Horse."

Caleb nodded as he digested and filed the name. "Running Horse, how many Crows ride with the Texas cattle?"

"Many. Bull Bear say half the warriors must go. Many Crow warriors, not many white cowmen. No fight."

Caleb smiled softly as they rode into the Texas cow camp and saw Jeff Chandler giving orders to his fanning-out riders. That was like old Bull Bear. He didn't want any fighting with the whites that would bring soldiers and swift retaliation, so he had shrewdly sent so many Crow warriors, armed and livid in war regalia, that the Texans would be awed and careful. Chandler looked at Caleb for a full minute as he rode up without saying a word. Running Horse reined away toward his warriors, scattered around the vast, horn-rattling herd, with a warning in Crow in an undertone: "Killer. Bad man. Silent Outcast, be careful." Doorn affected not to hear and nodded to Chandler, who sneered and whirled his horse and abruptly rode away, leaving Caleb alone.

The drive was a bedlam of noise. The Texas cattle were half wild and cagey. Bellowing, rattling their great horns, and drumming a dull rumble over the soggy prairie, they moved out after the unexpected rest with the energy of 2,000 demons. For the first five miles, the Texans and Crows alike were kept busy turning back bolters and lining out leaders on the dim, washy trail that led into the cañon. The sky was as clear as a bell, but the warmth had not yet come out with the new sun.

The cañon loomed up before them about ten o'clock, and the Crows made a sort of funnel out of themselves that steered the Texas cattle onto the narrow, slippery trail ahead. By the time the herd had gotten to the cañon, however, most of their surplus energy had been consumed and they were, for the most part, content to follow the critter ahead and leave the bolting and dragging to the tail end of the herd. They moved over the treacherous ground with calm acceptance and the Indians led them along at a mile-eating, long-legged walk.

With the drag came Jeff Chandler, swollen-faced and as touchy as a sidewinder, several Texas drovers, Running Horse, about thirty Crow warriors, and Caleb Doorn. The drag was reluctant about following the other critters into the pass, and it took a little maneuvering. In the course of the endeavor, Caleb's big black horse nudged Chandler's flashy sorrel. The Texan's rabid eyes came up shooting fire as Caleb apologized and rode on along the trail. Chandler quirted his way up behind Caleb. The trail was too narrow for their horses to get abreast.

"Ya done that apurpose. Ah seen it. Rubbin' in your piece o' luck, ain't ya, squawman!" Caleb bit back the gorge that arose within him and didn't answer. The men were well along on the trail by now, Caleb directly behind the cattle with Chandler behind him, Chandler's riders behind their employer and the silent, impassive Indians behind the Texans. Chandler's anger increased when Caleb ignored his taunt. "Damn squawman! Get daown offen that horse an ah'll beat ya to death fer what ya done yes'tiddy."

Caleb didn't move until Chandler's screaming oaths were accompanied by his whistling quirt that cut through the butternut shirt and brought a quick rush of blood through the torn flesh. He was off his horse in a second and, as Chandler's startled mount leaped forward, caught hold of the big man and yanked him bodily off the saddle. Chandler hit the ground with a roar of rage and dropped his quirt. Caleb was suddenly very white-faced. Whichever man went down this time would very likely pitch to his death off the narrow trail and into the cañon far below where a faint, distance-muffled roar told the men on the trail that the rain had swollen a small creek to a torrential river.

Caleb heard a growled, guttural snarl behind him. He darted a quick look as Chandler rushed him. The Crows, slit-eyed and venomous, had their rifles poised and aimed at the nervous cowboys in front of them. Stealing the look at the enemies behind him almost cost Caleb his life. Chandler knocked him down by sheer body weight. He could feel the steel spring fingers grabbing at the cloth of his clothes. Chandler wanted to lift him high and throw him into the cañon. He rolled and twisted frantically to avoid the tremendous bulk of the larger man. Hot, fetid breath was on the side of his face and he looked into a pair of bloodshot, rabid eyes. The shattered nose was beginning to drip blood from the violent exertions. Caleb flung up one arm and struck the Texan high on the head. It overbalanced Chandler and Caleb heaved mightily to complete the loss of balance. Springing up with the speed of a snake,

Caleb crouched, waiting. Chandler, remembering how he had been chopped down while getting to his feet the day before, rolled backward before rising.

There was no reckless confidence on the big man's face now. He was white with a seething hatred, but his eyes were diabolically cunning. Doorn circled a little, staying away from the edge of the trail. Chandler roared an oath and charged. Caleb met him desperately, braced and doggedly set. His fists flashed out like pile drivers. Still the Texan came in, slowed a little, but still reaching for a handhold that would enable him to throw Caleb into the cañon. Again the hard fists popped and ricocheted off the driving hulk of bone and muscle. This time Chandler, hurt, stopped and swung. The blow swooshed through the air and Caleb rolled his head. Still, the knuckles flashed past his ear with a tearing sound and the scout felt his blood running down over the torn shirt. He dropped low and rolled his shoulder with a slashing uppercut that sunk solidly into the big man's stomach. Chandler's eyes opened wide for a second and he gasped hoarsely, stepping away with a wobbly lurch.

Caleb, fighting the fight of his life, cold and unmerciful, moved in to follow up the injury done by his last strike. The Texan was looking anxious now, his face beaded in small, luminous drops of agonizing sweat. He threw out a massive arm to ward Caleb off. Caleb started to slide under it and slipped in the mud. He went down flat on his face, instinctively rolled sideways toward the edge of the cañon trail just as Chandler's boot smashed into his unprotected ribs. A fuzzy red shroud began to descend over his sight. An awful stitch of pain shot through him when he tried to breathe. Chandler roared a gasping, desperate cry of victory and threw himself on the prone, half-conscious form of the scout. Doorn rolled away from the edge of the trail by instinct. Consuming waves of nausea were coming up out of his bowels and sweeping over him. He locked his teeth and fought against them as he came groggily to one knee. Chandler, missing his victim with his body's throw and roll, clambered up to his knees, wiped the thick, heavy mud from his hands and face, then lurched to his feet as Caleb straightened up.

The frontiersman's fists felt like lead weights as he forced them out defensively. The stitch in his side was making him desperately sick and he bent almost double to get relief. Chandler, recovered from his own abuse, was smiling triumphantly as he came in slowly, teeth bared through the puffy flesh of his face. The little eyes, sunken and overshadowed by the mounds of injured flesh, were vicious, like the eyes of a murderous weasel confronting a helpless victim, livid, anticipatory, and merciless.

Chandler was swearing in a husky undertone. The voice was the only sound on the high trail overlooking the gorge below. Somewhere, far ahead, the bellowing of cattle floated back to the rigid watchers. The monotonous profanity was even and regularly spaced. Caleb watched the big body coming in. He planted his feet and forced himself almost erect, catching his breath with the effort. There could be no maneuvering or side-stepping now. His legs were rubber and his lungs were bellows of tortured, outraged flesh. Chandler was almost close enough now. Caleb forgot some of his agony in the desperation of what was ahead. Suddenly the big man lunged forward. The leaden fists swung methodically, one after the other. Caleb had the very rare ability of being able to hit as hard with one fist as he could with the other. Chandler rushed against the bruising knuckles. He pushed in trying to beat aside the pummeling fists, but they came through the air like the pendulum of a gigantic clock of bone and muscle. He slowed a little and still the fists slashed and jarred and thudded. He stopped altogether, a sob in his throat, swinging his own massive arms. Still the desperate, persistent knuckles smashed into him. His face was struck again and again and his head snapped back savagely with each blow. Now his mouth was open and a gorge of blood swelled out of it. Caleb took a step forward, still swinging with that ghastly, ashen look of the damned in his half-blind eyes. Another step forward and Chandler's big arms slowed and finally fell to his sides. Caleb walked forward, flat-footed, and fired all that remained in his body, one tremendous, earth-jarring swing that would have torn the head off a lesser man. Chandler was out on his feet, but he took an instinctive step backward to escape the next blow, which could never come. It was one step too far, and his great body suddenly disappeared over the edge of the trail as Caleb went slowly down to his knees, shaking his head lollingly from one side to the other, fighting doggedly for the consciousness that was slipping from him, driven by a subconscious urging that was warning him insanely of a peril that no longer existed.

Sally and Jack Britt were drinking their second pot of coffee when Caleb opened his eyes. The red film was gone, but the side ache was a biting, searing jolt of agony with each breath.

Britt looked down at him anxiously. "How ya feel, Caleb?"

"Alive, but in small pieces."

The grizzled old cowman sighed loudly and looked weakly over at Sally. "Alive, he says, girl."

The deep violet eyes were big in a pale, scared face. "It was awful." She caught the warning glare in Britt's face and swallowed hastily. "They way you ruined those new clothes, I mean. Why, that butternut shirt is nothing but shreds and, well, I don't know whether I'll ever be able to get all that mud out of those trousers or not." It wouldn't hold together. Sally's bravery crumpled like wet paper and she went down on her knees beside the bed, burying her face in the quilts over Caleb's bruised and aching body.

Britt cleared his throat in embarrassment. "Say, Caleb, uh, do me a favor, will ya?"

"Sure, Jack, what?"

"Dammit, the next time ya gotta fight with someone, make it a little guy, will ya? Why, that ox outweighed ya close to seventy pounds." There was a brisk thump on the back door and Britt started in his tracks, dropped his hand to his holster, and swung it open with a savage frown.

Bull Bear was standing there with a brand new fringed hunting shirt. He held it out ruefully and looked at Britt's hand on his holstered gun. "No good. Bull Bear always get almost shot when he come in here. No good." He smiled at Caleb and tossed the handsome shirt on the bed. "Running Horse send this shirt. He said you best fighter he ever seen. Some fight, by damn!" He turned abruptly and walked away.

Jack closed the door with a sigh as Sally raised her tear-stained face and looked at the Indian shirt. "No, Caleb. You've worn the last one of those things you're ever going to wear. From now on you dress like Jack an' the rest of the respectable cattlemen. The frontier is changing. You have to change with it." She tossed the fringed shirt into a corner and looked appealingly at Britt.

He cleared his throat again. "Uh, Caleb, uh . . . well, Sally an' I've bought you a little herd o' cows. Uh . . . like I told ya once before. Scoutin's all over, pardner. It's goin' to be cows from now on, not buffalo. Uh . . . you can buy a chunk of land an' be a cowman. Uh . . . how about it?"

Caleb looked sadly at the hunting shirt, over at Sally's wide, pleading and tear-stained eyes. He nodded to Britt. "I reckon you're right, Jack. From now on I'm a cowman."

Feud on the Mesa

I

There was a place called Purgatoire by the early trappers who came exploring across the Rockies, and the trappers, who the Indians did not kill or who were not assimilated into the plains culture, returned back where they had originated. When the next westering wave arrived, they were Yankees, called mountain men, instead of *voyageurs* as those earlier explorers had been called, and the Yankees turned Purgatoire into Picketwire.

Roughly the same thing happened upon the high, vast plateau above the New Mexico northwest cattle country, except that there the matter of corruption had a better, at least a more comprehensible genesis and evolution. For example, the first Spaniards to climb to the great plateau arrived there at a time of year when some contiguous areas beyond the immense sweep of pale grass were turning a tawny shade of reddish tan after the first light frost, and they consequently called the mesa Canela, which referred to the color of those sumac bushes as being cinnamon.

Then those lean horsemen passed along, wearing their fine casques and their leather armor, and several generations later the unarmored and much less hawk-like descendants of Spanish miscegenation rode up onto Canela Mesa, and in their imperfect, Indian-Spanish, called the mesa Canana, corrupting the Spanish name into something more relevant to them; they were also soldiers and explorers, and each of them carried a *canana* that contained their bullets. It was a little leather box that the French called a *cartouche* and that the next wave of newcomers—Yankees again—called a cartridge box, unless of course they were officers, then they used the French word, *cartouche*, because it sounded finer.

Finally a barrel-chested, black-bearded, fierce-eyed dauntless man named Amos Cane arrived on the mesa with his Shoshone wife and their string of pups ranging from panther-like youths in their teens to a baby on a travois behind a gentle, spotted-rump horse, and spent a golden summer creating a fortress-like big house of logs, an even larger log barn, outbuildings for smoking meat and storing things like salt and flour and dried wild fruit, a blacksmith shop and a bunkhouse for the half-wild youths, and the name Canana underwent another change. The high plateau became Cane's Mesa, and it remained known as Cane's Mesa after Amos, old and bowed with wars and labors, yielded up the doughty ghost, his tribe scattered to the four winds, and finally his *klootch* was also tamped down into the rich earth at his side, and the last of their offspring, a quiet, sober-eyed, golden-skinned woman of twenty-five named Elisabeth for some foreign queen her father had admired, but called Corn-flower by her mother because of her intensely blue eyes, was all that remained of the clan on Cane's Mesa. She was the one who had come up the tortuous trail out of the inferno of a New Mexico desert lashed to a travois.

There still was no other permanent resident on Cane's Mesa, although far-ranging cattlemen had been encroaching a little at a time, like wolves, as old Amos had become less able to mount his war horse, gather his sons with guns in hand to chase them away, and two summers after Elisabeth had buried her mother out back beneath the magnificent old cottonwood trees, within the little iron paling fence where old Amos also lay beneath his granite stone, a cowman named Arlen Chase had ridden into the yard, had sat his horse looking around at the massive old log buildings that were beginning to show signs of neglect and decay. When Elisabeth had come forth from the barn, he had told her bluntly that he was there to stay, and had stepped off his horse—right into the barrel of a horse pistol that had belonged to old Amos and had nine notches upon its stag-handled grips.

Arlen Chase hadn't stayed after all, but he had not left Cane Mesa, either. He had established his cow camp three miles northwest, close to where the ancient trail led off the mesa down to the lowland country, where it endlessly meandered until it came to the village—now the town—of Clearwater.

Chase's obvious intent was to block access to the mesa. He was a lifelong free-graze cowman and knew a valuable asset when he saw one. Cane's Mesa ran for roughly fifteen miles east to west, and from the northward high mountains to the sandstone, rusty red bluffs southward, it ran another six miles. A man would never have to overgraze Cane's Mesa to grow rich up there. All he would have to do would be to claim it and hold it. With that thought in mind, Arlen Chase hired riders who were more than range riders. Anyone could become a range rider, which required little enough talent, the Lord knew, but the other attributes Chase's men possessed only came from being courageous and willing, and fiercely loyal. Most range men regarded loyalty as a primary virtue; they existed in a world of feudal concepts and convictions, but the surest way to strain a man's sense of loyalty to the brand he rode for was to engage in activities that went against a man's moral grain.

The men Arlen Chase hired were never moralists. If Chase chose to blockade the pass and inaugurate a quietly passive siege of that black-haired, blue-eyed woman in the clutch of old log buildings who never went anywhere without a gun that she could use as well as any man, that was entirely agreeable to his riders. They made jokes about it, and once in a while, with or without a little firewater inside them, they would swoop in close to the old buildings and let fly a few rounds into the mighty log walls, not with an intention of shooting the woman, but simply in order to see her race for her house and grab up an old rifle to fire back. It was something that endlessly amused them even though they had learned early that it would remain a source of laughter only as long as they remained well out of gun range. She was an astonishingly unerring marksman, and, while they respected her for that, it made the little impromptu attacks all the more zestful. They were a wild breed of men. Arlen Chase never made a point of enquiring into the past of his riders; he only insisted that they work hard and obey orders, which they usually did because that was how they had matured, but from time to time it was said, down in Clearwater, that, if there'd been any law in the New Mexico-Colorado border country beyond an occasional town marshal, Arlen Chase's cow camps would have provided a jailhouse full of fugitives.

For Elisabeth, imprisoned upon her mesa, existence was little different from what it had always been. She worked hard at keeping her band of horses where the grass was best, and, although her cattle had been steadily diminishing in number for several years, since even before Arlen Chase had squatted on the mesa chasing away all other encroaching cowmen, she tried to keep track of them, too.

Once, she had hired two riders down at Clearwater. They had lasted three weeks; subsequently one of them turned up in Chase's camp, and the other one left the country never to return. After that, although she had tried to hire other men, none had ever arrived at her ranch. Not even the ones who had promised to ride up.

If they hadn't been discouraged down in Clearwater, then they had been halted where the trail came up atop the mesa. Chase's camp over there was a series of log corrals, some rough log structures thrown up in haste and with no genuine interest by his cowboys, who did not like that kind of work, and an area of trampled earth and dead grass that covered about thirty acres of land. There was a fringe of trees along the mesa's three borders, but down along the rusty old cliffs to the southward there was not a tree, just some scraggly underbrush that kept the sandstone from eroding too badly. Old Amos had often said they should plant trees there, for otherwise the cliffs were going slowly to wash away, but nothing had ever been done about that. There were always too many other things requiring more immediate attention. Planting trees, like planting anything else in the soil, was something old-timers either left to their young ones and womenfolk, or did themselves only when there was nothing else to claim their attention. And there was always something else; pioneering a land was nothing that could ever be accomplished in one man's lifetime. The best old Amos had been able to achieve had been his buildings, his family and its roots into the good soil of Cane's Mesa, and his armed defense of his private fief. Those things he had done well, but no man's accomplishments outlast him by very much, any more than his dreams outlast him.

For Elisabeth Cane, it was a concern of silent irony that only she—a woman—had fully inherited her father's strong, almost mystic love of the mesa. Five brothers had gone away, but because of a different course, they had learned to love, and, although Elisabeth had never learned that, she was a woman and she, therefore, understood it.

One of her sisters lived in Texas, married to a slow-drawling, gentle-acting, tough cowman who had come through on a trail drive. Maybe once a year Elisabeth would receive a letter from Texas. Her other sister had simply gone away. One night she had kissed Elisabeth, the youngest, and in the morning she and a fine chestnut horse were gone. Elisabeth had been unable to understand such a thing. When she had asked her mother, she'd been told simply that people were like the leaves of autumn, something within them blew them this way and that way; sometimes they came to earth in a stony, sere place, and sometimes they fared better, but whatever their destiny, its source lay within them, a personal thing.

Her mother had grieved. So had Amos who had been rapidly wearing out when that disappearance had occurred, but of her two parents Elisabeth had always felt that her mother's feelings were the deeper, even though her mother was nowhere nearly as articulate as her father. He could thunder and roar and hurl challenges, and he could, as when her sister took the chestnut horse and rode out to find her own individual world, suddenly become softly still and thoughtful and surprisingly gentle toward his woman. He did not lack feelings; he simply had a very difficult time expressing them, explaining them, and, when he tried, as when he wanted to say something soft to Elisabeth, or any of his children, it came out gruffly.

All the memories were there, on Cane's Mesa, in and around the massive old log structures. For Elisabeth, who had inherited from her father the soul sensation for her birthright, her heritage and the land where both still existed, and who had inherited from her mother a deep sense of almost fatalistic serenity, there was no other place.

If Arlen Chase triumphed finally, he would have to bury her out beneath those cottonwood trees inside the iron fence, and until he triumphed—when she thought about it at all, she was willing to concede that he probably *would* beat her and take over Cane's Mesa—until that happened, she would concede him nothing whether he slowly stole all her cattle and horses, slowly cut her off and starved her out, or whether through a miracle she survived Arlen Chase.

It was springtime when she rode and discovered Chase's horses, wearing their AC shoulder brand, running with her own horses. One week later she found her sole remaining bull dead in a shallow arroyo, shot cleanly between the eyes.

II

Springtime on top of Cane's Mesa was an amalgam of Colorado's last frosts and cold nights, and New Mexico's Santa Anna winds that came dryly hot in a swooping updraft along the scored faces of the red-rusty sandstone bluffs, pushing back the cold a little, yet not strong enough themselves to impart their curling heat.

The grass fairly jumped out of the ground. The trees around the grasslands brightened, and, if they were hardwoods, they came into full greenery complete with the downy cotton from cottonwoods, and the pollinated buddings from all the other varieties. It was the beginning of the best time of year, because neither the northward ice fields nor the southward infernos ever more than weakly met upon Cane's Mesa, which was what made summertime there, and late autumn, and even most winters as perfect for people as well as for livestock.

When a pair of horsemen cursed and grunted and scrabbled their way up atop the mesa from the west, and passed through a mile of solid pine and fir forest, clambering around ancient deadfalls nearly as tall as a mounted man and longer than most village roadways, then came to the thinning last fringe of dark trees to catch their first view of the mesa's huge rolling to flat grasslands, it was probably like getting from this life to the next one, at least for men born and bred to the saddle and to stockmen's ways.

They just simply reined down and sat there, like struck dumb, bronzed and weathered, faded and hard-eyed carvings, until the one called Jud said: "Now this is what a man spends his life dreaming about, and knows damned well don't exist."

The other man smiled, looped his reins so the horse could rest after his recent three-hour odyssey of travail, with scratched shins and seared lungs from the climb, and pointed.

"Smoke, Jud. Early for supper and late for dinner, I'd say."

Jud studied the distant, very faint tendril rising almost arrow-straight against the pale, flawless sky and made his guess. "Branding. It's that time of year again." Then Jud swung from the waist to look behind, but if there had been a troop of cavalry back through the dark forest, or a whole band of feathered war whoops, he couldn't have seen them because sunlight never reached fully to the forest's floor, and the trees stood thickly as hair on a dog's back.

When Jud straightened back around and caught his partner's sardonic smile, he shrugged. "I don't want it put on my headboard that they caught Jud Hudson from behind."

The smiling man turned back to gazing out where that faraway smoke arose. "No one's any closer behind us than the Gila Valley, and that's a month's damned hard riding back yonder." The speaker lifted his reins. "Want to bust right out, like we got a right?"

Jud considered. He was heavy boned but not heavy in build. He probably *would* have been heavy, if he'd had that chance, and, in fact, throughout all his thirty-five years he'd never had a chance to vegetate.

His partner was finer boned, leaned-down, sinewy as old rawhide and perhaps ten or fifteen pounds lighter, but he looked as weathered, as faded, as though he were about Jud's age. His name was Rufus Miller, and he was wanted back across a moonscape of desolation, of deadly desert and ghostly nights, for the same crime Jud Hudson was wanted for— stage robbery.

Jud hung fire over the decision on whether to ride forth boldly in plain sight or not. A month of trailing by moonlight and becoming shadows by sunlight had fixed in Jud Hudson a habit of reticence. He gestured. "We could stay among the trees and get most of the way down there."

Rufe turned to follow after, but, as he rode and studied this huge plateau, it became clear to him that, when they ran out of forest to protect them, they were going to be miles southward of that standing smoke. It also struck him that down south where those trees played out, there had to be a series of damned near perpendicular bluffs, because he could see 100 miles straight outward and downward without a single blessed knoll or ridge to interrupt the view.

Rufus Miller was a calm, pensive man, gray-eyed, capable, range-born and rough-raised. Earlier, like Jud, he had let his spurs down a notch in the towns so that they would make music on the plank walks, and he'd worn his gun in a special holster, twisted slightly away from his hip. But a man gets over those things—if he manages to survive his youth in a country where every other gun-carrying rooster is just as quick to make, or accept, challenges.

Rufe had survived and so had Jud, but they'd done some things others who had also survived had not done, like raiding the coach in the Gila Valley. But again, if a man can survive his errors and doesn't repeat them, there's hope for him.

There was not a worthwhile man alive who hadn't done his share of wild, senseless things. Unless he *had* done them, he never quite acquired the cross-hatch of invisible scars upon his inner self that, when he finally matured, made him wiser than many, more careful than most, and more understanding than the mill run of folks.

And that lousy stagecoach had turned out not to have one damned mail pouch on it. Nothing, not even a good watch, because the only passengers had been an old man and his little bird-like, frightened wife, and, hell, a man wouldn't take an old man's watch right there in front of his wife. Likewise the driver. He'd had three $10 gold pieces he'd been hoarding to buy his boy a speckled pony for Christmas.

They had ridden away fast, and empty-handed, and from the first high hill they had seen the cowman posse boiling up dust in flinging pursuit. So— becoming outlaws hadn't proven any more profitable than mustanging had been, or than range riding had been, or than horse-breaking had been, except that outlawing created reverberations, and they hadn't dared go back west of the Gila country where they'd been range riding, so they kept heading northeast, skirting around the worst of the desert country profanely assuring one another that the whole damned planet couldn't be that bad. And now, by God, it turned out that the whole damned planet *wasn't* that bad.

Jud drew rein, stepped to earth, peered steadily out across the golden sun smash, then turned and beckoned for Rufe to join him. "There's a big old log ranch out there, all by itself. That's where the smoke's rising up . . . out back behind the barn where the corrals are. You see?"

Rufe saw. The air was as clear as crystal glass, so the Cane place looked two miles closer than it was. Even so, those mighty log structures would have been visible from an even greater distance.

"That," announced Rufe, after thoughtful consideration, "is a pretty big outfit."

Jud said: "But the fire isn't. Maybe they only got one or two riders."

Rufe started back for his horse. "In that case, they sure need a couple more, this being marking season."

Jud went to his horse more slowly, inhibited by all the days and nights of secrecy and hiding. They understood one another better than brothers. Rufe leaned atop his saddle horn. "Jud, this can't last forever. Anyway, we're so far off even if those cowmen were still trailing us, their damned clothes'd be out of style by the time they got over this far. And those folks down there probably never even heard of the Gila country."

Jud wagged his head and climbed back across leather looking worried, but he offered no objection when Rufe struck out past the final tier of huge old shaggy trees into the dazzling sunlight, heading for the log buildings. They had a considerable distance to cover. That clear air did not delude them, although they had been traveling through it this time of year all their lives, going one place or another. In fact, limitless horizons had from boyhood conditioned them both, and a large army of similar men, to half believe that the traveling was the important thing, that goals, or the arriving at some destination, were for people who had to have goals.

They were two miles closer when Rufe said: "Things have been better for that outfit." It was finally possible to note the signs of gentle neglect and decay, the patched corral stringers, the weeds flourishing along the back of the huge old barn, the bare places up above where winter wind had carried away fir shakes in patches, letting rainwater drop straight through to the barn's interior.

Jud stood in his stirrups, hat brim pulled low, and said nothing until he eased down, then he sighed. "One man at the branding fire in the corral, Rufe. This time, we'd have done better to stay in the trees." He turned slightly, movement far out catching his attention. He raised an arm. "Three riders. Maybe they've been hunting more cattle to put into the corrals."

Rufe looked, saw those three horsemen suddenly haul back to a sliding halt and stare hard down in the direction of Rufe and Jud. "Must not get many strangers up on this mesa," Rufe said, watching those three distant horsemen, and Jud's reaction was wary.

"We shouldn't have left the damned forest."

The three riders came on, more slowly now, in an easy lope, erect in the saddle with an unmistakable, sharp interest. Jud yanked loose the tie-down on his holstered Colt and leaned to loosen his Winchester in its boot.

Rufe watched, said nothing for a long while, and, when he finally turned in the direction of the log barn and those old log working corrals, he saw a hatted dark head come up over the topmost corral stringer. He also saw sunshine dully along gray steel.

"Caught between the rockslide and a hard place," he said quietly. "Look yonder, Jud, at the corral."

They had little choice, being completely exposed out on the grasslands, but to keep right on slowly riding toward the buildings. Whatever they had stumbled into, they were certainly not going to be able to shoot their way out of, so the alternative had to be talk.

Jud said: "Sure a fine day for sighting down a rifle barrel. That feller in the corral doesn't have a carbine. He's got a rifle. If he's any kind of a shot, he could knock my hat off from right where we are now."

Rufe, watching the three horsemen, swore quietly. "Damn it all, they're fanning out. This is like riding into a nest of Apaches." Rufe kept watching the riders. They fanned out, for a fact, but the closer the pair of strangers got to the buildings, the less those three riders seemed inclined to come closer, and that didn't make sense to Rufe. If he and Jud had stumbled onto some old mossback's private domain where trespassers were badly treated, it seemed that his mounted men would cut off all retreat and herd the strangers down that other fellow's rifle barrel.

Rufe tipped down his hat, rubbed his jaw, and finally said: "Jud, there's something wrong here. You know what I think?"

"Right now," replied Jud, alternately squinting at the rifle barrel resting atop a corral stringer and those three distant horsemen, "I'm not interested in what you think, unless it's got to do with us cutting back and making it to those damned trees before we get shot."

Rufe was scowling. "I don't think those horsemen got anything to do with that feller in the corral with the rifle. I think they're deliberately staying beyond his range."

Jud leaned a little also to study the range men, and in fact it was at about this time that they hauled to a halt, conferred briefly, then one man stepped down from his saddle, shielded by the other two, so that neither Jud nor Rufe could see what he was doing— until he fired.

Rufe's stocky little bay horse, a companion of many a hard trail, as honest as the day was long, gave a huge lunge high into the air, folded all four legs, and dropped, stone dead.

Rufe barely had time to kick his feet free before he hit the ground, rolling, the wind half knocked out of him, dimly hearing Jud's roar of rage as his partner rolled from the saddle dragging out his saddle gun, but those distant riders were already turning tail.

Jud fired three times, elevating his sight each time, and cursing with helplessness because no carbine could reach that far.

From the corral, that rifle roared. It had a sound like a light cannon, and, because its range was much greater, Jud lowered his weapon to watch. But the horsemen were also beyond rifle range.

Jud stood up, looked from the dead horse to his partner, who was sitting there blinking and feeling around for the ground in order to push upright, then Jud turned in the direction of the corral and saw that rifle still trained in the direction of those fleeing horsemen. He shook his head in complete bafflement, stepped over, and lent Rufe a hand.

"You all right?"

Rufe picked up his hat, said nothing, went over and leaned down to put a hand upon the bay horse's neck, and after a moment, still saying nothing, he straightened up, gazing far out where the racing range men were still in the easterly sun blaze.

III

She was long-legged for a woman, and flat everywhere hard work made people flat, but she was also round in all the places Nature made women round. She had thick, absolutely straight, black hair in two braids past her shoulders, very dark blue eyes, and skin the color of new cream. She looked to be maybe twenty or twenty-two, and not even the boots, the faded trousers, the old work shirt, and the streaked old wide-brimmed hat could detract from something else men immediately noticed about Elisabeth Cane. She was beautiful.

But beauty being a relative term, even to men who had not see a beautiful woman—*any* kind of a woman at all in over a month—that rifle she held as steadily as stone as they stiffly dismounted from riding on in, both upon Jud's horse, made her beauty less immediate than the bronzed hand on the gun, with one bent finger curled around the trigger.

Jud was still sulphurous, so he said: "Lady, point that gun some other way."

She did not move and neither did the long barrel. "Who are you?" she demanded.

Rufe, glancing back where his horse and outfit lay, spoke slowly when he came back around facing her.

"My name is Rufus Miller. His name is Jud Hudson. We were just riding through."

"Up through that badlands country from the west?" she said, eyeing them skeptically as her father and brothers had always eyed men coming onto Cane's Mesa from that improbable direction.

"Yeah," said Rufe, looking steadily at her. "Up through those badlands. Is there another way up here?"

She did not answer that. "What do you want?"

Jud said: "Well, until about fifteen minutes ago, we didn't want anything, lady, but that was before some son . . . that was before a feller shot Rufe's bay horse."

The gun barrel tipped down a fraction, and the hard blue eyes above it studied both men. "I'll sell you another horse," she said. "Sound, well broke, and cheap. Then you had better turn and go back exactly the way you came. There's an easier way off the mesa, but you'd never make it."

Jud's anger never departed quickly. He looked back harshly at the handsome woman. "Is that a fact, ma'am? Why wouldn't we ever make it?"

"A cowman named Arlen Chase has a camp over there. He has four riders. All five of them. . . ."

"Wait a minute," broke in Rufe. "Is that who those three fellers were . . . riders for this Arlen Chase?"

"Yes."

"Do they own this mesa, ma'am?"

"No. I own it. But they control it now because . . . well, there are five of them, and they are men, and, even when I've gone down to Clearwater to hire riders, they never show up, or else they get chased off." The gun barrel tilted a little more toward the ground. She studied Rufe a moment before saying: "The man

who shot that bay horse from under you, mister, is
named Charley Fenwick. I know them all by sight,
from far out." Elisabeth turned and pointed with the
rifle. "Those are bullet holes fired into the barn by
Chase's men. I've got them in every building, even
over in the house walls. But they come in very fast,
just ahead of sunlight, or right after dark, usually
when I'm choring." She grounded the rifle and
leaned on it. "I wear a six-gun, but I can't work with a
rifle in one hand, can I?"

Rufe sighed and slowly turned to look more closely
at the buildings. Jud fished out a tobacco sack and
went slowly to work making a cigarette, his bronzed
features locked down in a clear expression of anger.
As he was lighting up, Rufe said: "What's your name,
lady?"

"Elisabeth Cane. This is Cane's Mesa. My father
settled it. He's buried yonder, inside that little iron
fence. So is my mother."

Rufe glanced at the corral behind Elisabeth where
about fifteen old cows with rough-looking, under-
nourished runty little calves waited uneasily. The
smoke was still rising from a stone ring where three
branding irons were heating.

"You do all this yourself?" asked Rufe.

Elisabeth's answer was almost curt: "Do all what?
Brand about a dozen sickly calves, all that's left of
my bunch?"

Rufe accepted the rebuke. "Yeah, I guess you could
do it." He looked at Jud, who looked darkly back,
then Rufe said: "Miz Cane, I can't go far on foot, and
Jud's animal is tired, and we're both in need of work,
so. . . ."

"I don't want you on the ranch," Elisabeth said

firmly. "There's not enough room inside the fence for two more graves."

"Now, lady," stated Jud, "I don't figure to try and squeeze inside that little fence, but for folks to go around shooting other folks' horses out from under them . . . you can hire us on, or we'll set us up a camp around here somewhere in among the trees, but either way someone's going to settle up for my partner's horse." Jud jutted his square jaw. "Is that the bunkhouse?"

Elisabeth did not turn in the direction Jud was looking. She simply said: "They will either run you off, or kill you."

Jud's answer was direct: "They haven't run you off nor killed you, lady."

Elisabeth had no answer, apparently, because she offered none as Jud stepped back to scoop up the reins of his horse and turn in the direction of the barn's big rear opening. To Rufe, who still stood there, she said: "You see those cattle? That's all I have left, and they shot my bull a week back, which means that next year even those old cows won't be coming in with calves at their sides . . . I can no longer pay riders, Mister Miller. There's just no money."

Rufe said: "Shot your bull?"

Elisabeth pointed. "Up there, about four miles toward the mountains, there is a deep arroyo. He's down in there, shot between the eyes."

Rufe stood a while gazing out and around, then he finally said: "Well, I might as well go back and fetch in my outfit. And if you've got some tools, I'd like to bury my horse. He sure was a good friend to me, ma'am."

She took him to the barn where Jud had already

off-saddled and was standing up front, leaning in the opening, smoking thoughtfully and gazing out over the great sweep of grass country. Jud strolled back to watch Elisabeth take down two shovels and hand one to Rufe. Jud watched her standing there, holding the other shovel, eyes widening.

He said: "You figure to go help Rufe bury his horse?"

She turned on Jud. "I figured to, because I didn't figure *you* would."

Jud stepped on his smoke and ground it out, then raised his eyes to her handsome face, and held out a hand, trying to smile. "I guess I did something wrong. I'm sorry. I don't want you for an enemy. By the way, where did you leave that old buffalo rifle?"

She handed him the shovel without giving any indication that she knew she was being subtly teased. "Put your nose where it shouldn't be, Mister Hudson, and you'll find where I leave that buffalo gun . . . I'll feed the critters, go make something for us to eat, and afterward we can work those calves. But you're wasting your time. I have no money, and Arlen Chase will either hire you away or run you out of the country." She turned and walked out of the barn toward the golden-lit yard, leaving two stalwart, faded men looking after her.

They went out and began digging. Rufe's little bay horse had been pigeon-toed, and mule-nosed, and slanty-eyed, and as dependable as springtime grass, but he also weighed just a shade over 1,000 pounds and was built like a stone wall, and, if the ground hadn't been warmly moldy, digging his grave would have been impossible without a stout team, a good set of chain harness, and a Fresno scraper. In fact, they did not finish it until that night, because they had to go eat when Elisabeth rang the bell, and, after eating, they had to rope and snub and overhaul those little shaggy calves.

They finished the grave by moonlight, rolled the bay horse in, and bleakly went to work putting all that earth back into the hole. They were almost finished when Elisabeth came out with two huge old crockery cups of black coffee, and, when they leaned on their shovels to express gratitude and drink, the coffee turned out to be laced strongly with whiskey.

Jud smiled for the first time all day, but he kept his thoughts to himself. So did Rufe. He thanked her, and considered her in the ghostly moonlight and star shine as something a man might conjure up in a dream sometime, as a sort of ideal woman, but he said nothing until she looked down at their work, and said: "My father told me one time that a man who would shoot an honest horse was not one bit better than a murderer."

Jud finished the coffee, passed back the cup, wiped his mouth on the back of a soiled shirt sleeve, and turned back to work. "Your father was absolutely right, ma'am. What did you say that man's name was?"

"The one who shot the horse? Charley Fenwick. He rode for me last year, for about three weeks, then he disappeared, and the next I knew, he was riding for Arlen Chase."

"And shooting folks' horses," added Jud, leaning into his work. "Tell us about this Mister Chase, ma'am."

She told them all she knew, which actually was not very much, because excepting that first time Chase had ridden into the yard to announce that he was moving in, and she had drawn on him, they had not met again face to face more than three or four times, and those other times he had taunted her but had not lingered after doing it. She told them how her cattle had dwindled from 300 head down to what was in the corral, and how the best of her horses had just simply disappeared. She said: "I mentioned this to a pair of cowmen down near Clearwater . . . older men who had known my father, and they said likely some Indians passing through up along the north-ward mountains had taken the horses. It's possible. One thing I know, Chase's men don't ride Arrowhead horses, and I brand foals as soon as I can catch their mothers."

"That's probably why they don't ride them," Jud suggested very dryly. "Awfully hard on a man's neck, getting caught riding a horse he doesn't have a bill of sale for."

She looked cynically at Jud. "Not on Cane's Mesa, it isn't, Mister Hudson. Who would hang them?"

Rufe grinned down at her. "You, more'n likely. You can rope pretty well, shoot pretty well. I figure you could also lynch pretty well."

She watched them, and never smiled, and after a while she turned and went back to the big old log house. They finished mounding the earth, hauled Rufe's outfit as well as the shovels back to the barn, then headed for the creek that ran from north to south on the east side of the yard, out a quarter mile or so, and got deeply into the willow thicket before they stripped down. Every now and then Jud would part the willows and look back at the lighted window in the log house. Finally, when Rufe stepped into the water and gasped, Jud said: "All right, you go first and I'll keep watch." He was standing back there naked as a jaybird except for his hat, swatting at mosquitoes. Rufe took another step, shivered all over, then gasped back an answer.

"You don't have to keep watch, for hell's sake. She's in the house, and, anyway, she don't even know we're out here."

Jud would not accept this. "Like hell I don't," he hissed. "She came up onto us over where we buried your horse, didn't she, and this is a sight worse."

Rufe did not argue. For one thing that innocent-looking water must have come straight down off some Colorado mountaintop that had ice on it all year around. For another thing, the mosquitoes, accustomed to having to feed off animals with thick coats of hair, were coming to the bathing hole in clouds, and, until Rufe finally got deep down into the water, they bit him mercilessly. Up in the willows Jud finally used his hat, and his sizzling profanity, to fight them off, and the hat worked fairly well, while the cursing did not help one bit.

Ordinarily they creek-bathed at the hottest time of day, then lay under a blazing sun to dry off. Tonight, they dressed while still dripping wet, then hightailed it for the bunkhouse, closing and barring the door after them as though those ravenous little flying creatures had the strength to open the door.

They fell into bed and did not even look up when a rooster crowed from the barn loft, did not stir until the sun finally listed up out of New Mexico, and shone across Cane's Mesa in Colorado.

IV

Jud rode out to drift back a little herd of horses that had appeared westerly a couple of miles. Elisabeth was sure they belonged to her, at least that some of them did, and, when Jud had saddled up, he had cast a long look at Rufe, who had said nothing, simply nodding his head.

But nothing happened. There was not another horseman in sight, and the day was another epic of golden fragrance and perfect visibility. A man could see for many miles.

They corralled the horses, Jud took his horse inside to care for him, and out where Rufe was leaning upon the stringers, gazing in, Elisabeth said all those AC horses belonged to Chase, and the ones with the Lance and Shield mark on their left shoulder belonged to her. Of the thirty-three horses, nine were Lance and Shield. Rufe was interested, and, while she was explaining, Jud ambled out to stand with them.

She pointed to a barrel-chested, handsome dun horse that acted a little like a stallion. He kept maneuvering himself between the other horses and the people, and would flatten his ears if another horse seemed about to move past him, in front.

"He's stagy," she said, "for a very good reason.

He ran at stud until he was seven. Now he's almost nine years old."

Jud leaned and slowly straightened up wearing a slight frown. "You altered him at seven, ma'am?"

She put a withering look upon Hudson. "Chase altered him, Mister Hudson. Do I look that green?"

Jud, catching Rufe's amused twinkle, rolled up his eyes as though in supplication. "Miz Cane, all I did was ask a question. How come, every time I open my mouth, you want to shove your fist down it?"

She gripped the topmost corral stringer with strong, tanned hands and stared stonily in at the horses for a long while, a battle obviously under way deep down. Finally she looked at Rufe, who was relaxedly watching her, then looked on past to Jud.

"I apologize. I . . . you're right, Mister Hudson, I've been downright rude."

For Jud, this was worse than being snapped at, so he pointed to a rather raw-boned dark horse and mentioned that one time, years back, he'd owned a horse with that build and color that had been tougher than a rawhide cannon ball.

The conversation got back to normal, which, for livestock people, was to a discussion of animals, horses or cattle, or the things that affected either or both, such as the weather, the prospects for a good season, and so forth. In the end Elisabeth, who had been leaning there studying that seal-brown horse, said: "You can have him, Mister Miller, if you want him." She glanced at the other horses. "He's a well-broke animal, and so is that sorrel mare with the flaxen mane and tail. So is the little chunky gray horse, but the others . . . I haven't had time even to break them to lead."

They moved to release all the horses but the brown one, and, when they closed the sagging old gate, confining him, he raced back and forth whinnying to his departing friends.

They went around to the front of the bunkhouse, which had been built to house Elisabeth's long-gone brothers, and sat in kindly shade beneath a warped wooden overhang upon the plank porch where two benches were dowelled into the wall, and where two handmade chairs showed the ravages of being left out in the weather through many harsh winters.

There, while Rufe tossed his hat down beside him upon the bench, disclosing a face Mexican-dark from the eyes down, and almost indecently white from the eyes up, Elisabeth sat in one of the chairs, and Rufe cocked back the other one, with his booted feet hooked over the railing as he said: "About that dun stag, out there, Miz Cane, did he just come in one day, altered?"

She explained. "I found him by himself under some trees, with a fever. They cut him in midsummer and the flies had maggotted him pretty bad, Mister Miller. He was sick, so I didn't have very much trouble driving him home, and doctoring him."

Rufe said: "In July, ma'am?"

She raised cornflower blue eyes. "Yes." Then she added the rest of it, because they were all livestock people and cutting a stallion then turning him out in fly time meant the same thing to all of them—a prolonged, agonizing death for a bleeding animal that could not really protect his wound from foul-smelling, inescapable infection.

"They knew what they were doing, Mister Miller, the same as when they shot my bull. The same as when they've somehow or other whittled me down to maybe a dozen horses and those few old gummer cows we worked yesterday. They're telling me what to expect."

Jud rolled a smoke and passed the makings to his partner. As though he hadn't been listening, he said: "Tell us about that town, down yonder."

"Clearwater? There's not much to tell. It's a stage stop. Once, a few years back, there was some talk about the telegraph coming in, but it never did. There are some log holding pens south of town, for when several cow outfits want to make the drive eighty miles to rail's end together. It has a big general store and so forth." She smiled faintly. "My parents used to make the trip by wagon. We'd start early one morning, reach town by afternoon, lie over, and head back the next day. That general store . . . around Christmas time when my father would read to us from a book he had about Christmas and Santa Claus and the North Pole where all those wonderful things were . . . well, I'd think of that general store."

Rufe smiled at her with understanding, but Jud pursued the topic from a quite different angle. In a drawling tone he said: "Clearwater's got a store, and a tradin' barn, and all like that . . . and a jail-house?"

Elisabeth agreed. "Those things, and a retired Army doctor named Bruce Tappan. It's a cowmen's town."

Jud understood. "Pretty wild on Saturday night, eh?"

She did not know about that. "I've never been in Clearwater on a Saturday night, Mister Hudson."

Jud looked at her, slightly startled, then dropped

his head a little and studied the flaky accumulation of ash on his cigarette.

Rufe arose with a rattling sigh. "Sure nice, here like this, but I figure I'd better ride out the brown horse so's we can get acquainted." He looked back. "You better trail along in case I need someone to pick me out of the grass."

Jud arose, and they sauntered down to the corral without a word passing between them. Elisabeth remained back on the porch, gazing after them, chin resting upon crossed arms atop the porch railing. She would have enjoyed going down there with them, and even saddling up and riding out with them, but years ago she had been inhibited against this very thing by perfectly blunt-talking brothers who had left no doubt in her mind at all about there being times when a man did not want a female around, at all.

Maybe this really was not one of those times, but she did not want to find out, so she sat there, watching, and, when the pair of range men left the corral heading northward, side-by-side, Rufe Miller riding the tough brown horse that she knew would give him no trouble, she wondered about them, wondered why, if they were range riders, they were this far south of the Colorado big country ranges, or this far north of the desert cow outfits.

It was entirely possible that they just had no intention of working hard this season. Frequently range men did that, took a summer off and just went poking and exploring around. And yet Rufe had said they had needed work.

She watched them grow small, far out in the sunlight with its barely discernible heat haze, and remembered the very casual way Jud Hudson had tackled the last three words on his question about Clearwater: *and a jailhouse?* The idea that they might be fugitives did not shock her. Ever since she could remember, she had heard her father speaking about men he'd encountered skulking through the yonder trees.

She had no illusions about outlaws; this was exactly the kind of out-of-the-way country they gravitated toward. Jud maybe, she told herself. He did not smile very readily and he had a look to him that she could not define, but that she felt hid something.

Rufe was different. She suddenly straightened up, frowned, then arose and went briskly down in the direction of the barn to hunt stolen nests in the loft and mangers, and rob them of eggs for a cake.

The heat haze was as faint as gauze but as obvious as the thin drift of blue-bellied clouds stringing out very slowly from the northwest. The weather could change. It was not yet fully summer and the combined natural complexities that locked in a predictable variety of summer weather southward over the New Mexican desert, and farther northward upon the peaks and parks of Colorado, had not completed that equinoctial meld yet. As a matter of fact, they never seemed actually to accomplish this in the vicinity of Cane's Mesa. When it had ceased to rain out over the desert, for example, and had not yet begun the summer rains in Colorado, it quite often rained on Cane's Mesa.

Undoubtedly this was what accounted for the thick profusion of stirrup-high grass that grew most of the year. That same eternal thermal conflict overhead was also responsible for the open winters when no snow fell, although anyone atop the mesa could see it falling just about every other place.

As Jud observed while he and Rufe rode northward and Jud studied those incoming thin clouds, a man could get pretty badly fooled, trying to guess the weather upon a plateau like this one, and Rufe, who was not particularly interested in the weather and had been watching the seal-brown horse's ears, made his pronouncement of satisfaction.

"He's not the little bay horse, but he'll do."

Jud thought so. "Tough and strong and savvy. All you got to do is pay her for him."

"With what? Anyway, she said she'd *give* him to me."

"Why should she do that?" inquired Jud. "It wasn't *her* gun killed your horse."

Rufe turned, scowling. "You're sure argumentative today."

Jud smiled. "Nope. I was just fixing to weasel you around until you figured out how to pay Miz Lizzie for the brown horse."

Rufe understood at once. "All right. What's on your mind?"

"A whole lot of things like cuttin' her stud horse when they knew he'd take a week to die, and shooting her bull, and running off her other animals, and shooting up her buildings, and. . . ."

"Damn it, I know all that stuff, too, Jud, you don't have to convince me!" exclaimed Rufe. "What's on your devious little goat-sized mind?"

"Maybe we'd ought to go down and visit that town," Hudson replied. "They got a jailhouse, which means they got a lawman. Seems to me, before we brace Arlen Chase, we'd ought to know what else we might be bucking into."

Rufe was disappointed. He had thought his partner had evolved some plan to hit back at Chase. "That's a hell of a long ride, down there and back, and it'll be just as damned uncomfortable going back down as it was getting up here."

Jud smiled again. "Not the way I figure for us to go. I figure for us to go right through Mister Chase's cow camp tonight, maybe about one or two o'clock in the morning, cut his picket pins, kerosene his flour, turn out his corral stock, then take on down the trail for town with him bawling bloody murder and runnin' around in his nightshirt waitin' for dawn, so's he can charge down off the mesa on our trail, which we'll conveniently leave as plain as day with shod horse sign."

Jud looked down. "You got to shoe that brown horse, Rufe."

Every man had some chores he preferred to other chores. Rufe preferred almost anything at all to horseshoeing. He groaned as they turned, heading back for the ranch.

Jud loped along as cheerful as a cherub. He usually became this way when his mind was busy. They had the buildings in sight when Rufe said: "Tell you what, if you'll shoe this horse, Jud, I'll. . . ."

"Like hell," chirped Hudson. "Whatever it is, I'm not going to shoe your horse. Besides, you're a better blacksmith than I am . . . Rufe, do you smell that?"

They loped almost to the farthest log corral and hauled down to a walk before Rufe, head up, nose wrinkled, gave his answer.

"Cake! By Gawd, Jud, I don't believe it. Now *that*

is what I call a female woman. Shoot, brand, bite your head off, and bake cakes."

They turned into the barn, unrigged, cared for their animals, and went up front to stand in the doorway with late day softening the sunlight around them, catching an even closer, more tantalizing aroma of oven baking.

V

They were at supper in the main house, scrubbed and shiny and as hungry as a pair of bitch wolves, when Elisabeth asked how Rufe liked the brown horse, and he told her he'd take him, and pay her as soon as he found a cache somewhere.

She was pouring Jud's coffee and looked over Jud's head to say: "I didn't *sell* him to you. I *gave* him to you." She finished pouring, put the pot down, and sat down at her place across from Rufe. "I told you there's no money for hired hands any more. The brown horse will be part of your pay . . . or just a gift, Mister Miller, because within another month or two he'll disappear anyway."

Jud said nothing. It was an idiosyncrasy of his that Armageddon could occur right outside the cook house window complete with winged, trumpeting hosts, and Jud would not look up or comment until he finished his meal. He did not speak now, when Rufe said: "I'll consider the horse part wages then, Miz Cane. He's a using animal. Didn't even make trouble when I shod him . . . which I had to do even though I've got a bad back, because my partner wouldn't help."

He winked at Elisabeth, but Jud ignored them

both. It had been a very, very long while since he
had eaten steak with hash-browned potatoes and
fresh-made coffee, all of it woman-cooked. One insult was certainly no deterrent.

Elisabeth smiled more, this evening, and it was
very becoming to her. Once she even laughed. That
was near the end of supper when Jud finally looked
up and around, with only his coffee left to be consumed, and said: "Your back never bothered you in
your life, Rufe. Ma'am, you mind this feller, he can
josh a bird right down off a tree."

She brought out the cake and put it upon the table.
The two men sat contemplating it with genuine ap-
preciation, and Elisabeth, like most young women,
made excuses.

"My mother was better with that stove than I'll
ever be. She used to say it had a personality, just like
a person, and the best way to get along with it was
never to get it too hot, and always keep it clean." She
pointed to a dip in the cake's top. "Well, I've always
done exactly as she said, and, look there, the cake
started to fall anyway."

She cut them each a huge piece, ate none herself,
and refilled the coffee cups, then sat and watched.
Again, Jud did not raise his face as long as there
were any crumbs on his plate. He only looked up to
protest feebly when Elisabeth cut off another great
slice and slid it onto his plate.

She did the same for Rufe, and smiled at him
when he said he'd known when they'd first ridden
in, yesterday, from the way she'd held that old buffalo rifle, that she was the best cook on Cane's Mesa.

"The only cook, Mister Miller, except for Abe
Smith, Arlen Chase's *cocinero*." She sat down,

thought a moment, then added more. "And I don't drink nearly as much as Abe does."

Afterward, they went out upon the rambling porch of the main house, and she told them stories of her father, of her mother and brothers. She even told them about the sister who had ridden off and who had never returned, or even written.

This fascinated Jud for some reason. Regardless of how their subsequent talk drifted away, Jud kept bringing it back to the mysterious disappearance of Elisabeth's older sister.

Even later, when the pair of men went down to the bunkhouse, Jud said: "Why, unless her pa beat her, or some cowboy got her in a family way, would a girl run off from up here?"

Rufe sighed. "What's so terrible about that? You've met kids with peach fuzz for whiskers from here to there, who ran off from somewhere."

"Boys," averred Jud. "Boys, and even some men . . . but she was a girl."

Rufe went to the door, opened it slightly to look out, examined the sky, the solitary lighted window over at the main house, and sniffed the air before pulling back to say: "I wish to hell she'd turn in."

That did not trouble Jud in the least. "She won't hear us if we lead the horses out a mile or so before riding off. Are you ready?"

They went down to the barn, led forth the horses, and methodically saddled up without a word, slung booted carbines under *rosaderos*, buckled throat latches, went up for a final look in the direction of the main house—where there was finally only darkness, indicating that Elisabeth had gone to bed—then they trooped on through and out the back way, walking as quietly as was necessary, leading their animals.

That veil of obscurity was still up there, across the high heavens. It dulled down the brilliance of the stars, and those lean clouds they had noticed in the afternoon had got reinforcements from up north and were now widening their scope and thickening their depth and height.

Rufe sniffed. "Rain coming, Jud."

They swung up a mile out, turned eastward, and picked their way, in no hurry at all. They had the full night ahead, and the later it was when they located Chase's cow camp, the better for their purpose.

But they didn't reach it.

Jud was rolling a smoke when Rufe's horse threw up its head, missed a lead, and pointed onward with its little furry ears. Rufe stopped, swung down, and lay a hand lightly upon the horse's nostrils to pinch off a nicker, if one started.

Jud dropped the cigarette two-thirds fashioned to do the same, but it irritated him, so he hissed a little profanity while they stood, peering out into the gloomy night with its steadily decreasing visibility.

A shod hoof struck rock. They placed the direction of that sound but saw nothing. Rufe leaned close to whisper. "Maybe Chase's remuda broke out."

Jud did not reply. He handed Rufe his reins and went ahead like a soundless wraith.

The night was warm, but it was hard to make things out, even against the ghostly paleness of the grass, and Rufe had misgivings, even before his partner returned and said: "Hell, it's three mounted fellers skulking along south of us, heading for the Cane place." He grabbed his reins and swung away to mount and turn back. Rufe was already in the saddle before Jud reined over close to lean and whisper again.

"I understood her to say they only shot up the ranch about sunrise and about sunset."

Rufe was straining to detect the southward, onward sound, and glared without comment. Jud subsided and rode with one hand on the butt of his holstered Colt. He did not need an answer to his comment, anyway. Unless those three riders were strangers, which seemed improbable since they were coming directly from the area where Chase's cow camp was located, they had to be some of Chase's men.

Rufe formed his own opinion while he was riding. Perhaps Elisabeth Cane's foemen only harassed her at sunup and sundown ordinarily, but now they knew she had two riders on the Cane place, and that might very well have decided them to stop the harassment and move directly against her. It was entirely possible that Arlen Chase had sent his men over to frighten Miller and Hudson off the mesa, or, if that failed, actually to make a serious raid.

As nearly as Rufe could figure it out from what Elisabeth had said, this private range war had been in progress for about two years.

Rufe did not know Arlen Chase, would not have known him if they suddenly met face to face, but he knew cowmen, and he had yet to meet one who was possessed of enormous patience. It was about time for Chase to make his move to take over the mesa and get rid of the last of the Canes.

He and Jud were slightly farther back than they could have been while Rufe rode along seeking to second-guess those quiet riders on ahead. The invisible men up ahead suddenly veered northward, and that puzzled both Jud and Rufe. The Cane place was southward and westerly.

At Jud's scowl of enquiry, Rufe threw up his hands. They turned, also, but now they began closing the distance a little, and, when the horsemen up ahead halted, it was not the abrupt atrophy of hoof falls that signaled this back to Rufe and Jud, it was a strongly resonant voice softly saying: "Remember, just the barn. And as quick as you've got it going, get the hell back here."

Rufe and Jud exchanged a look, then turned off southerly, riding very quietly at a steady walk down through the matted grass on an angle that would put them between Chase's men and the Cane place.

They did not actually have very much ground to cover. Chase's men, who they had detected and followed, had been on the right course up until they had veered northward, so Rufe and Jud had simply turned back in the direction from which they had originally ridden out.

They made no particular attempt to determine whether all three of those range riders, or one or two of them, were actually going to try and reach the Cane barn. All they really had to know was that someone was heading for the barn, and the way that man with resonant voice had said it, neither Rufe nor Jud was required to possess perspicacity to guess what he had been talking about. Burning someone's barn was a very old act of enmity in the range country. It was also very fatal if a man was caught in the act of doing it.

They struck out at a slightly swifter pace once they had plenty of distance between them and Arlen Chase's riders. The barn's high hulking silhouette emerged from the night on their right, and they reined over there, swung off, and led their horses inside where it was like off-saddling in the depths of an ink bottle.

They conversed only once, very briefly, after the horses had been stalled. Rufe said he would watch the front if Jud would watch out back, then they briefly mentioned the advantage of being practical instead of heroic, and parted with a couple of hard smiles.

The night was as hushed as death, and to Rufe, up near the front of the log barn, whose visibility in the direction of the main house where Elisabeth was blissfully slumbering was totally unimpeded, it seemed most probable that those skulkers—one, two, or all three of them for all he knew—would enter the barn from out back. It did not especially worry him that Jud was alone back there. The interior of the old barn was almost Stygian. Jud had a great advantage—none of Chase's men knew there was an ambush established—and, finally, Rufe knew for a fact that an angrily aroused Jud Hudson was the equal of just about any two cowboys west of the Missouri.

He listened, relaxed a little with one hand on his holstered Colt, and was reflecting upon Arlen Chase's strategy—which, to Rufe Miller, appeared needlessly prolonged—when he heard what sounded like the rub of two bits of dry wood, one against the other.

He eased just a fraction more in the direction of the wide front opening and detected the sound again. It was someone's leather boot soles gliding with infinite care across gritty soil, and it was close by, perhaps slightly south of the front barn opening, but not as far down alongside the log wall as the rear of the barn.

He drew his Colt, thinking that he had been wrong; they weren't going to slip into the barn from out back, after all.

It was a fair guess, considering he had only heard one sound, that of a man in boots approaching on an angle in the direction of the front of the barn. What changed his thinking was when a man with a carbine in his right fist gradually emerged from the darkness moving to the northeast corner of the barn and halted there, leaning almost comfortably, gazing in the direction of the main house, and also in the direction of the log bunkhouse, which was within the man's same visionary perimeter.

The man put carbine against the side of the barn, fished forth a plug of twist, gnawed off a piece, pouched it into one cheek, put away what remained of the twist, then nonchalantly lifted his carbine again.

Rufe guessed now that this man was someone else's bodyguard. He shot a swift look down through the blackness toward the back of the barn. Since the second man did not appear out front, he undoubtedly would be around back. Rufe had no misgivings. Jud was more of an Indian than Rufe was; he would take care of the other one.

Rufe tipped up his pistol barrel, stepped across through the blackness on the balls of his feet, eased around, and without haste projected his entire body out into the night gloom along the front of the barn, no more than twenty feet from that calmly chewing man with the carbine hanging loosely over one bent arm, and cocked his six-gun.

That little, muted but unmistakable sound made the slouching cowboy's rhythmically moving jaws suddenly freeze. The man did not move anything but his eyes. He saw Rufe, saw the cocked gun aimed straight at his stomach, and seemed momentarily to stop breathing.

Rufe smiled and said very softly: "Not one sound."

VI

The night was serenely velvet, endlessly quiet, and, except for that tiny space in the vault of the night where Rufe disarmed Arlen Chase's cowboy, there did not seem to be even so much as a mote of discord anywhere in the universe. He shoved the cowboy's carbine and Colt away with his boot toe from where they were standing, asked the man quietly if he had a belly gun or a boot knife, got a headshake, then said: "Where's your friend?"

The cowboy answered in a half husky whisper. "Out back."

"To fire the barn?"

The cowboy nodded.

"The third feller . . . where is he?"

The cowboy's eyes widened in surprise. "Holding our horses. How'd you know there was three of us?"

Rufe ignored the question and motioned for the cowboy to sit down. The man looked warily at the cocked gun, evidently believing the worst, but he obeyed; he sat down with his back to the log wall— and Rufe chopped hard downward, driving the man's hat over his ears with the pistol barrel. The cowboy loosened all over, then gently toppled sideways.

Rufe returned swiftly to the black interior of the barn, heading through as soundlessly as he could.

When he saw the opening, he knelt low, then peered out. Jud was invisible. Rufe surmised he probably was around the corner of the barn, and stood up to ease out into the lighter gloom, then halt and listen. Eventually he heard something. It could have been simply an animal out beyond the corrals drowsily moving, or it could have been a man around the corner alongside the barn's north wall. He started around there and was almost to the corner, when he heard a soft voice say: "I ain't moving, mister."

He stopped and waited. That hadn't been Jud's voice. For a moment there was no sound, until his partner growled in his familiar way, then Rufe called quietly: "Jud, you got him?"

The answer came swiftly in the same growling tone: "Yeah, the son-of-a-bitch's got a bundle of rags soaked in coal oil."

Rufe walked on around. This range man was tall, half a head taller than Jud but only half as thick. Even if Jud hadn't had his Colt ten feet from the rider's middle, it was unlikely that Chase's cowboy would have been Jud's match.

The cowboy looked from Jud to Rufe, then back again. He was both badly shaken and frightened. In the poor light he also looked guiltily uncomfortable about the wad of smelly rags in his gloved left fist.

Jud leathered his weapon and ordered the cowboy to drop the oil-soaked rags, which Chase's man did, then Jud stood glowering while Rufe asked if the man's name happened to be Fenwick. The cowboy said: "No, sir, my name's Smith."

Jud sneered. "Mine's Santa Claus."

Rufe had another question. "I knocked your friend over the head out front. Is his name Fenwick?"

"No sir," replied the cowboy, sounding believable.

"Charley didn't come in. He's out yonder holding the horses."

This was all Rufe needed. He turned slightly. "Fetch some chain from the barn, Jud. Let's lash these two, then go find Mister Fenwick. He owes me for the bay horse."

After Jud had hiked back toward the barn opening, Rufe studied their prisoner. He was not only tall and thin; he did not look to be more than perhaps twenty years old. He also looked worried.

"You ever see what happens to men who burn folks out?" Rufe asked, then pointed upwards where a pole rafter extended from the barn's sloping roof. "Folks hang them."

The cowboy involuntarily glanced upwards, then down again very quickly.

Jud returned, dragging some chain harness. Without speaking, he pointed earthward and Chase's man sat down so that Jud could chain his arms behind his back, and lash his ankles with the same length of trace chain. When Jud finished, the subdued cowboy was helpless. Unless someone came along to release him, he would rot right where he sat. There was no way for him to get free.

They went around front where the other man lay on his side. Jud leaned and pulled the man up into a sitting position, propped him against the barn, then knocked his hat away to see his face as he said to Rufe: "Maybe you killed the bastard."

But the man groaned, so Jud sighed, then returned to the barn for another set of chain harness. The man did not rouse until Jud had returned and was roughly chaining his arms and ankles exactly as he had done with the other night rider. Finally, when it was done and Jud arose to knock dust from his knees with his hat, the man opened his eyes, feebly groaned again, and gradually focused his sight upon the two lean men gazing dispassionately down at him. When he tried to move and the chains clanked, he looked down at his ankles.

Jud said: "Hope you don't get too cold before we bring Mister Fenwick back to join you."

The captive raised his eyes to Jud's bitter face, unwilling to speak until Rufe put a question to him.

"Who's left at Chase's camp with you three fellers gone?"

"Abe, the cook, Arlen, another of the riders, and some whiskery feller who rode in today from down at Clearwater."

Except for the man from Clearwater, all this jibed with what Elisabeth had told Rufe and Jud. They were interested in the newcomer and asked about him. But the cowboy did not seem to know much.

"I think Arlen met him down in town couple of days back. He said his name was Bull Harris. That's all I know. Him and Arlen went around together today. They didn't come over where the rest of us was. Then Arlen called us in tonight and told us to come over here. . . ."

"And burn the lady out," growled Jud.

The cowboy, eyeing Jud warily, nodded his head very slightly. "Yeah."

Rufe picked up the carbine from the dust and jerked back the slide to reveal a shiny brass casing, slid the breech closed, and looked at Jud. Without a word they started away.

The cowboy called softly: "Supposing you don't make it back?"

"Then you'll likely catch pneumonia," replied Jud.

"But that's better'n the hanging you'll get if we *do* come back."

They knew about where Charley Fenwick, the third Chase rider, was waiting with the three horses. They also knew he would be as wary as a fox, and for that reason, when they got two-thirds of the way out there, with those silently swelling high clouds beginning to coalesce and blot out more starlight, they split off, one going to the left, one to the right.

It was not hard to skyline the horses even in the deepening gloom, because one of them was gray— someone's oversight; no night rider in his right mind would ride a gray horse on a dark night, if he did not want to be detected.

Rufe was to the east, to the right of where he and Jud had split up, and, as he started directly westward in the direction of that gray horse and the pair of darker lumpy silhouettes standing with the gray, he palmed his weapon while still holding the Winchester. The range was too close for a carbine. He walked another few yards, halted, dropped to one knee, and for a long while remained that way, separating silhouettes up ahead in an effort to define the one belonging to a man.

Suddenly someone softly called. "Smith? What the hell happened? I don't see no fire."

Jud answered, and Rufe thought he was lying prone because his bitter words appeared to rise up from the earth. "You son-of-a-bitch . . . make one little move and I'll kill you."

There was no way to mistake Jud's earnestness. Rufe waited, but the dim shape ahead of him, facing away, standing a scant foot or two in front of the drowsing horses, took root.

Just to lend support to Jud's bitter order, Rufe

cocked his Colt exactly as he had done before, so that the sound would chill the blood of the man whose back was set squarely to Rufe.

It worked. The silhouette stiffened and froze in place. Rufe called over: "He's all yours, Jud, if you want to disarm him!"

The cowboy waited until Jud was walking on up, then showed a different temperament from the other two, when he said: "Mister, you're making one hell of a mistake. Chase'll bury you on this mesa, and you won't be the first he's caught out for helpin' that damned 'breed woman."

Jud said nothing. He disarmed the man, and, as Rufe walked up, Jud looked at him. "Rufe, this here is Mister Fenwick. Mister Fenwick, I'd admire for you to meet my partner, Rufe Miller. It was his bay horse you killed day before yesterday, and to be right honest with you, Mister Fenwick, I wouldn't want to be standin' in your boots right now."

Rufe studied the range man. Charley Fenwick was a little heavier, just as tall as Rufe, and did not show fear at all when he turned from Jud toward Rufe. "That was your first warning," he stated. "Tonight was to be your second warning. That's all Arlen Chase gives, two warnings . . . then he buries you."

Rufe smiled as he ambled on up. When he swung, Charley Fenwick was looking him squarely in the eye, perhaps aware that trouble was on its way. But Rufe was as swift as a striking snake. His blow grated bone over bone up alongside Charley Fenwick's cheek bone, on up past his temple, and into his hair. The hat flopped outward, then fell, and its owner staggered, blinked rapidly, let out a roar of pain and fury, and backed away.

Rufe did not go after him, which was a mistake. The blow had only temporarily stunned Charley Fenwick, who was a rugged man of iron will and stamina. He swore at Rufe, rolled up his shoulders as he started forward, fists cocked, and, when he was close enough, he launched himself like a muscle-and-bone projectile, which was the standard procedure among barroom brawlers. He also sprung his arms wide, like a bear, obviously intending to lock them around Rufe's back.

Rufe did not yield an inch of ground. They came together with violent force. Fenwick's impetus would have compelled a bull elk to give ground. Rufe was braced, legs sprung wide, but he still had to yield a little even as he fired blow after blow into Fenwick's unprotected middle, and Rufe was one of those desperately lanky, sinewy men who had surprising strength and power.

He did not yield another foot, nor did he seem to be heeding the roars and wild punches of his adversary as he steadily went to work battering away at the heavier man's soft parts.

Jud was standing to one side, arms folded, grinning from ear to ear. He had seen this happen before. Rufe possessed a unique ability; most men who were so lightning fast lacked power. Rufe was very fast, *with* power. He practically smothered the heavier man with blows that hurt, beginning low and working his way upward, until Fenwick, gasping, had to give away, had to try and get away from that raining punishment by retreating. But Rufe did not allow this. Each time Fenwick would throw a punch, then step back, Rufe would ward off the strike, then step ahead, fists flailing.

He had been struck several times, and Fenwick

was one of those individuals whose blows, slow in arriving and not accurately sent, were bone bruising when they connected.

Rufe would have mottled flesh on his body for a week after this fight was ended, but right at the moment, when he was landing five-to-one with his adversary, he was conscious of very little actual pain as he concentrated on downing Charley Fenwick.

Then, unexpectedly, Rufe paused, dropped both arms, and jumped clear. Fenwick's mouth was torn and his lower body was racked with pain. His eyes, partially glazed, still showed the smoke haze of battle, though. He raised a bruised fist to push off the blood from his chin, and waited.

Rufe said: "Jud, give the son-of-a-bitch back his gun."

Jud's savage smile froze. "What? What are you talking about?"

"Give him his gun, damn it. This isn't pay enough for my little bay horse. I'm going to kill him."

Jud did not move for a while, but eventually he uncrossed his arms and scowled. "He can hardly stand up, Rufe. He ain't a match for a little old lady, right now." Jud ambled over, cocked his head at Charley Fenwick, then without warning swung savagely from the buckle. Fenwick's head went violently backward, his legs turned loose, and Fenwick fell.

Jud did not even turn as he leaned down. "Give me a hand pitching him across one of their horses, and let's get back to the ranch."

VII

By the time they got back to the barn and unceremoniously dumped unconscious Charley Fenwick in the dirt, Rufe was well aware that he had been pummeled by a man whose blows had sledge-hammer power.

Without a word to the chained man propped out front, who watched their arrival with a slack jaw, they yanked loose the rigging from the three Chase horses, turned them into a corral, then prodded the tall youth who had been in possession of the oil-soaked rags up to his feet, and kept prodding until he had crow-hopped the full distance around front—where he saw the dirty, torn, and bloody lump lying a few feet in front of his chained companion. The tall youth sank down beside the other prisoner, round shoulders against the barn's front wall, staring.

Jud went after a bucket of water while Rufe rolled a smoke, lit up, flexed his aching hands, and completely ignored the prisoners until Jud returned, and hurled the bucket's full, cold contents upon Charley Fenwick. He was rewarded with a weak spluttering sound, a small fit of coughing, and that was all, so Jud upended the bucket, sat down upon it, and joined Rufe studying their pair of chained captives.

After a while Rufe put forth a question. "You boys

think it's funny as hell, charging by here firing into the buildings, don't you?"

The lanky youth swallowed hard, and turned to the older rider, but the older man was already wary, so he did not answer, either. The youth looked up at Rufe. "No, sir, it ain't funny."

"Then why did you do it?"

"Well. . . ."

Jud snorted in disgust. "I never figured Chase, or his men, any different. Anyone who makes war on a woman alone is plumb gutless." He looked longest at the older cowboy. "We're goin' to maybe set you loose, one at a time, give you back your guns, then my partner'n me'll take turns bucking you . . . hand-guns only."

The cowboy said: "Wait a minute. Personally I never aimed low. I'd shoot high along the walls. And I never really liked this way of doin' it. If Chase wanted her out, all he had to do was come right on in some night, tie her up, and send her out of here, belly down, on one of the pack animals."

"Sure," agreed Rufe. "Or send you fellers over to burn her out."

The cowboy paused, licked his lips, then grudgingly nodded. "Yeah. But, hell, even that's better'n maybe accidently shooting her, ain't it?"

Jud cast a sidelong glance at Fenwick, lying soggily in the darkened, wet dirt. As he glanced back, he said—"I'll get a rope."—and arose off the wooden bucket. "We can hang the young feller last . . . but we can't hang this horse-killing bastard until he wakes up. That leaves just this other one for now."

The youth made a small sound deeply in his throat, then he strained on the chains. The other cowboy looked over, a little sympathetically, and a trifle scornfully. "You always run the risk of not succeedin'," he mumbled. "I told you that on the ride over."

Rufe dropped his smoke and ground it underfoot. He did not look at either of the prisoners until Jud came back out of the barn, lariat in hand, then Rufe faced the tall, thin younger range man.

"How old are you?" he asked.

"Twenty."

"Where you from?"

"West Texas . . . sir . . . an' my folks are church-abidin' folks of the Baptist faith, and I never in my life done nothing like this. . . ."

"Sure not," growled Jud, looking blackly at the youth. "You know some prayers, Baptist boy? You better start reciting them for you and your big, brave, woman-fightin' friend here."

The older cowboy eyed Jud steadily. "He's telling you the truth. We picked him up last winter down in town when we needed someone to mind the horses, chop wood, and help haul water for the *cocinero*. He's the least feller Chase ever had with the outfit. Hell, he ain't old enough to have done much, is he? Well, then . . . figure he's learned a lesson and let him loose."

"So he can ride back to Chase and tell him what happened over here?" growled Jud, shaking out a loop, then snugging it back to begin making the eight-inch wrap for a hangman's knot.

"I won't!" exclaimed the tall youth. "I swear I won't. I'll head west, mister. I won't even *look* easterly. And I'll keep on riding. I give you my word. I swear it to you!"

Jud continued to manufacture his hangman's knot, acting as though he had not heard a word the youth had said. Then he stepped over close and began peering upwards as though seeking an eave end with enough of a notch or knot to it so that the rope would not pull off.

It was Rufe who finally spoke to the boy. "The penalty for burning folks out is the same as the penalty for stealing their horses or rustling their cattle. Did you know that when you left Chase's cow camp tonight?"

The youth struggled with the truth for a long while. All three older men watched, all three of them mightily curious about how he would answer. Then he said: "Yes, sir, I knew that."

Rufe nodded. "But you didn't really figure to fire the barn, is that it?"

"No, sir, that ain't it. I figured to fire it, like Chase said we was to do. I figured . . . burn her barn, and maybe next time her house . . . and she'll leave without no one getting hurt very much."

Jud asked: "And if you had a mother or a sister living alone, and some range scum came along to burn them out?" Jud did not wait for an answer; he had found his eave, and twisted to flip the rope expertly up and over, and catch the tag end when it came dangling down.

The older range man watched Jud making the adjustments. After a moment of this he glanced up at Rufe. "Mister, if you'll fish in my pocket, you'll find some Kentucky twist, and, if you'd hold it up so's I could get a chaw, I'd be right obliged."

Rufe leaned down to get the man's chewing tobacco, and, when he was that close, the cowboy said: "Hell, he's only a kid . . . scairt two-thirds to death . . . and he didn't really *do* nothing, anyhow."

Rufe held out the twist, the cowboy gnawed off a

corner, and, when Rufe shoved the plug back, then straightened up, he and the older man looked stonily at one another.

Rufe stepped away, reached to yank the tall youth to his feet, whirled him roughly against the barn, face forward, then yanked loose the arm chains with Jud standing off a short distance, watching from an expressionless face.

Rufe spun the youth back to face him and said: "Sit down and take the ankle chains off."

The cowboy sank down almost as though his legs could not support his spindly frame. He fumbled with the chains while all three older men eyed him. When he was free at last, Rufe said: "If you go anywhere even *near* Chase's cow camp, or if you go down to that town on the desert and hang around down there . . . or if I ever see you again at all, you're going to get shot all to hell. *Get!*"

The youth stared, so Jud repeated it. "*Get!* Damn it, climb onto your hind legs and commence running westerly. On foot. Mister Chase'll have the law on you if you make off with one of his horses. Now *get!*"

The lanky youth spun and fled around the side of the barn. They could still hear him fleeing, one long stride after another, for some little time.

Jud hauled down the lariat and coiled it slowly and thoughtfully. He did not look at the remaining prisoner, not until he had the rope ready to be re-slung from a saddle swell, and snapped it against his legs a couple of times. Then he glanced over. "How about you, mister?"

The cowboy's answer was quietly offered. "I guess I got to set here. If you ain't going to lynch me, why then I expect I'm just going to have to set here."

Jud looked over at Rufe, shrugged, and went over to lend a hand at boosting the rider onto his feet and shoving him along into the barn. This one was not a boy, and evidently neither was he a liar. He could have told the same kind of story, but he hadn't done it. He was a typical range man: loyal.

He made no secret of it, but by the time he had done this, he had also obviously decided that Rufe and Jud had never intended to hang anyone.

They shoved him down in a pile of hay and left him there, walked out front, eyed Charley Fenwick, and got the chains they had used on the youth to chain up Fenwick. He was beginning to come around when they boosted him up and hustled him down to the same pile of hay, and let him fall. He even muttered some profanity as he rolled and came to rest beside the other rider. Then he looked around. It was just as dark inside the log barn now as it had been two hours before. Maybe it was even darker, although it was hard to tell when a man's eyes could absorb just so much darkness.

Rufe took Jud out back where they lit up and relaxed in the warm, pleasant night. Those overhead clouds had surreptitiously been broadening, deepening, and thickening ever since sundown, until now, an hour after midnight, they had most of the sky blocked out. And they were low clouds, the kind that normally were rain-swollen.

But the air did not smell exactly right, yet, which Jud commented on casually as he stood, smoking and gazing upward and around as though this was the only thing on his mind.

Rufe flexed his right hand several times, listening to his partner's comments upon the possibility of rain, then he raised a skeptical pair of eyes and said: "When you get it all sorted out about whether it's going to rain or not . . . let's ride."

Jud turned. "Where?"

Rufe looked sardonic even in that dismal, ghostly darkness. "Chase's cow camp. It won't be the dice table at Tucson, but it's a hell of a lot closer."

"What about those fellers in the barn?"

"They're not going anywhere," said Rufe, still working his knuckles to loosen them, and keep them loose. "And if you're worrying about Miz Cane comin' out to gather eggs in the morning and finding them there . . . well, they'll be worse off after that meeting than she'll be."

Jud sighed. "All right. But . . . oh, nothing. Let's get to riding."

They went back inside for their horses, and, although the chained prisoners could make out most of what they were doing during the process of saddling up, neither side spoke to the other side.

When Jud walked his horse out front, then swung astraddle, that lowering sky was seemingly frozen in place. It did not appear to have increased its rain cloud encroachment at all over the past hour.

In the direction of the main house there was still hushed darkness. This time, as Rufe and Jud left the yard, they did not bother being shadowy about it. In fact, Jud lit a cigarette behind his hat before they had quite cleared the far environs of the yard, and settled back in the saddle looking ahead and off to his left, completely assured that things at the ranch were as they should be.

Rufe, seeking some approximation of the time, searched for a moon glimmer through those fish-belly clouds, and had no success whatsoever. He surmised, though, that it had to be perhaps about two o'clock in the morning.

The only reason that time might be relevant was because he and Jud wanted to hit Arlen Chase's camp at the quietest time of the night, for even though anyone who might be sitting up over there, listening and waiting, might think oncoming horsemen would be the arsonists returning and would therefore be unlikely to ambush Jud and Rufe, it was Rufe's opinion that under these circumstances a man needed all the help he could get from a dark night, from a mistaken listener, and of course from a benign fate—if there were such a thing.

It was a good thing they had been able to get a good night's rest the previous night, Jud said, as they rode along, because, sure as hell, they weren't going to get any sleep tonight. He also said he had a feeling that if they could keep on hitting Arlen Chase as they had been doing, they just might accomplish something.

"He's likely lyin' in his bedroll sleeping like a baby, confident his boys came over, fired the barn, and rode off clean. Instead, we got the three of them. With some luck, we'll get him while he's sleepin' too." Jud smiled through the darkness. "Hit him hard and often, Rufe. Never let him get his feet square under him. How's that sound for strategy?"

Rufe laughed. "Great. Tell me something. Smart as you are, how's it come you didn't become a general in the Army?"

Jud made a gesture. "I figured a little on it, you

see, but blue ain't my color. Always made me look like I got dark bags under my eyes, so I chose range ridin' instead."

Rufe snorted in derision, and Jud leaned over his saddle horn, laughing.

VIII

They had to retrace their earlier route and beyond for several miles, and, while they had every reason not to expect another encounter as they'd had earlier, they were within a mile or so of the mesa's eastward rim when they distinctly heard horses again.

This time, though, it turned out to be animals in a large corral. In fact, when they finally got up close enough to make the animals out, it appeared that the corral was almost a small pasture. It looked as though its post-and-rider fence encompassed three or four acres of land.

The cow camp would be somewhere beyond this enclosure, so they left their horses tied in a clump of second-growth jack pines and reconnoitered forward, fanning out a little, but doing this in a manner that allowed them to sight each other all the while they were moving stealthily forward.

There were no lights. If someone was awaiting the return of Arlen Chase's night riders, he was doing it in darkness.

They finally made out a structure. It was crude and low-roofed, the walls made of rough logs that had not been fitted very well, and between were liberal coatings of mud plaster.

They came together and considered this building. It looked like either a large storage house, or perhaps a bunkhouse. They split off, each man coming around toward the front of it from one rough side. When they met out front, they had their answer. It was a storehouse. If it had been Chase's bunkhouse, it would not have had that huge iron hasp and lock on the outside of the door.

There were several other buildings, and one in particular held Rufe's attention. It was longer than the others, and a mud-wattle chimney arose above the east wall. Rufe tapped his partner's arm. "Cook shack," he whispered.

Jud agreed, and offered a suggestion. "Yeah. By rights Chase's old dough belly ought to be sleeping in there. Want to look?"

They went carefully around the building in utter silence and starless gloom, found a door ajar whose leather hinges were on the verge of wearing through, and without a sound walked inside.

The table was long and an iron stove stood against that distant east wall with its stovepipe shoved up the mud-wattle chimney. They divided the room between themselves, with the long gang table in the center, and went step by step along until they came to the cook stove and, beside it, the big kindling box. Here, wooden pegs in the log wall held every size of cooking pan and cow-camp utensil, suspended downward. Here, too, they found a wall bunk behind a flour sack partition with a lumpy, bedraggled-looking shape in it, peacefully sleeping. Jud remained beside the bunk while Rufe went on along to complete their examination of the cook shack. He stood longest beside a window that overlooked the main yard.

What puzzled him was that no one at Chase's cow

camp seemed to be awaiting the return of the night riders. Of course, there could be many reasons for this, including the basic one which suggested that no one *had* to wait up for men sent out to do a job no one thought would amount to anything more than riding up, sneaking in, setting the fire, then loping for home.

Rufe turned back, and, when he stepped behind the flour-sack partition, he saw an awry-haired older man sitting straight up in bed, wide awake, his long john underwear pale in the darkness to match his beard-stubbled face, and Jud standing above the old man, smiling wolfishly downward. When Rufe stepped from behind the flour sacks, the man in the bed jumped his astonished stare to Rufe. He was obviously nonplussed. Since he had never seen either of the armed men standing at his bedside like a pair of wraiths, he had reason to be nonplussed. Also, his conscience might have had something to do with it; those two lanky men eyeing him in the silent night did not look as though they had arrived to commend him for his dumplings or his crab-apple pies, and, like most older range men, this one, whose name was Abe Smith and who was Chase's camp cook, had not dedicated his total lifetime to altruistic pursuits.

Rufe said—"Where's your gun?"—and the old man did not so much as hesitate. He pointed to a pair of pack boxes that doubled as his chest of drawers.

Jud leaned, shoved a hand under the pillow, and withdrew it, empty.

The old man said: "The only gun I got is yonder in them boxes." He looked from Jud to Rufe as though he had in mind asking a question, but he said nothing.

"Where's Mister Chase?" Rufe asked quietly, and got an unexpected answer.

"Him and Mister Harris done rode out for town just ahead of sunset."

Jud leaned down. "You're lying."

The cook vehemently shook his head. "I ain't lying, mister. Him and Mister Harris left for town just ahead of supper. They figured to spend the night down there."

Jud continued to lean close, staring at the cook. "Maybe you're not lying, you old bastard. Maybe they sent Fenwick and his friends over to fire the Cane barn, then lit out for town so's folks would see them down there when the barn burned down." Jud smiled again coldly. "Does that sound reasonable, you old bastard?"

The cook fidgeted. He was over the astonishment now, and it seemed rather clear that normally he was an irascible man, quick-tempered and sharp-tongued. But whether he liked the deliberate way Jud referred to him as an aged illegitimate or not, fidgeting seemed right at the moment to be about as far as he had ought to go in registering a protest. He said: "I don't know why Mister Chase and that gun-fighter went down to Clearwater. I'm only the cook here. Folks never confide in cooks. They bellyache to high heaven if the grub ain't served up hot and on time, and fit for a king, mind you, but otherwise a cow-camp cook might just as well be a. . . ."

"Shut up," murmured Jud, still leaning down. "How do you know Harris is a gunfighter?"

Abe Smith hung fire, looking left and right a moment before answering. "Well, hell, I know it the same as you boys'd know it if you seen him. They got a special look to 'em, don't they?"

Jud nodded solemn confirmation of this. "Yeah, you old bastard, they got a special look to 'em. What kind of a man is Chase, to hire a gunfighter to kill the Cane woman?"

Abe Smith snorted. "Not *her*, for Chriz' sake, *them*. Hell's bells, a man don't hire a woman killed, he. . . ."

"Yeah? He what . . . old bastard?"

Abe Smith's sudden spurt of indignant denial had been entirely impromptu, so he sat there looking up, cursing himself in silence, because now, finally, he knew exactly who these two strangers were—the very men Chase had hired the gunfighter to kill. Abe Smith watched Jud straighten up very slowly, and, although this act was not of itself at all menacing, the overall attitude of both the lanky men in the darkness beside his bed definitely was menacing. It was no good, relying upon rangeland custom of old men being safe, unless the old men knew with whom they were confronted. Abe Smith did not know, and, furthermore, these two armed strangers shouldn't even have been able to get over here. They were supposed to be fighting a barn fire and maybe getting shot at by Charley Fenwick and the others.

Abe said: "Do you boys work for Miz Cane?"

Rufe answered. "You answer, you old bastard, you don't ask. Finish what you were going to say about the gunfighter . . . Chase hired him to kill . . . who?"

Abe Smith swallowed, hard. "Well, he hired Harris to get rid of them two range riders workin' for Elisabeth Cane."

Jud cocked a skeptical eye. "I thought you said no one confided in you?"

"No one does," averred the older man. "But that don't mean, when I'm feedin' 'em all, I don't listen a lot. Otherwise, hell, I'd never know nothing. I'd be like one of them monks who folks don't never talk to."

Rufe exchanged a look with Jud. It was a disappointment, not being able to find Arlen Chase, but it was also helpful to know who the man Bull Harris was, and why Chase had brought him to Cane's Mesa.

Rufe said: "Who else is in camp tonight, besides you, old bastard?"

Abe Smith fidgeted a little more furiously this time. "One feller over in the bunkhouse, which is that log house bigger than the main house, but beside it and off a dozen yards. His name's Pete Ruff, and he's sort of the straw boss when Mister Chase ain't on the mesa."

Rufe gestured. "Get your boots and pants on, and let's go over and rouse up Pete Ruff."

Abe Smith swung spindly, saddle-warped legs clad in ancient long johns over the edge of his bunk, groped for trousers and boots, gruntingly dressed himself, scooped up his shirt, and arose. Standing up evidently made him feel a little more like a two-legged critter, because he looked Rufe squarely in the eye and said: "You *are* them two from the Cane place, ain't you?"

Jud tapped the old man's shoulder and growled: "Shut up, lead the way, and the first mistake you make, old bastard, I'm going to bust your skull like a punky melon."

The cook clumped out through his cook shack into the warm, heavy late-night atmosphere, did not look back and did not hesitate as he struck out directly for a particular crude log house. This one had a little overhang out front, several crude benches, and a wooden box held empty beer and whiskey bottles.

Rufe reached and halted Abe Smith with a hard grip. "Poke your head inside, yell for him to come out, that the horses are spooked about something, then stand over against the wall and don't move nor make a sound. You understand?"

The cook nodded, and reached for the door. When he shoved his head inside, Jud's cold gun muzzle eased into his back above the kidneys and Abe Smith flinched. He growled loudly for the sleeping man to rouse up and come out and help him quiet the damned horses, and he swore a little, which made it sound very authentic. Then he stepped over alongside the wall and flattened exactly as he had been instructed to do.

The man, who came sleepily forth buttoning his britches with a disreputable old hat upon the back of his tousled head and clutching a shirt under one arm, was dark-haired, dark-eyed, and with a slightly hawkish face. He could have been a half-breed Indian of some kind, but whatever he was, Rufe's first good glimpse of him encouraged a belief that *this* member of Chase's cow camp was trouble.

Not now, though. He not only had both hands occupied, but he was unarmed when Jud stepped up and shoved the cold gun barrel into the man's side. Ruff turned in swift astonishment and stared. Jud was a complete stranger to him. He seemed unwilling or unable to speak for a moment, but only that long, because when Jud said—"Turn around and go back inside, mister, and keep both your hands up high."—the cow-camp range boss recovered and glared at Jud.

"Who the hell do you think you are?" he snarled.

Rufe answered, from behind the man. "Go inside!"

The range boss had not been able to make any kind of a worthwhile assessment until now. He turned his head and craned around, saw Rufe, and decided he was, indeed, outmatched. Then he curled a furious lip in the direction of old Abe Smith, but whatever he might have said was cut short when Jud jammed him hard with the gun barrel, making the range boss gasp as he turned to reënter the bunkhouse.

They turned up the lamp inside. Ruff shrugged into his shirt, staring quizzically at his captors. Abe Smith confirmed the range boss's dawning suspicions.

"They're the pair Elisabeth Cane hired on couple days back."

Pete Ruff looked at Rufe. "What you doin' over here?"

"Looking for Arlen Chase."

"He ain't here. He ain't nowhere on the mesa," snapped Ruff.

"Yeah," retorted Rufe, "we know. He's down in Clearwater with his gunfighter. Well, directly now we're going to ride down there and look him up, but first off we've got to make blessed certain no one's behind us, skulking along for a chance to back-shoot us."

"How you figure to do that?" asked Pete Ruff.

Rufe shrugged. "Kill the pair of you, like we did those other three, the ones you sent over to burn the lady's barn."

Old Abe Smith acted as though he were going to faint, and even the hard-eyed, tough half-breed range boss turned suddenly much less hard and abrasive.

"It wasn't my doings," said the half-breed. "Mister Chase come up with it, lock, stock, and barrel. I never even picked the fellers to ride over there." He turned toward the cook. "Is that the truth, or not, Abe?"

Smith's voice was reedy when he replied: "Don't you ask me nothing. I'm just the. . . ."

Jud growled and Abe's lips snapped closed as Rufe offered them a way out. "You can ride down to Clearwater with us, tell the law down there what Chase has been trying to do up here . . . steal her horses and cattle, burn her out, shoot up her place . . . or you can get buried right here."

Abe Smith hardly allowed the last echo to fade. "I'll go with you, by Gawd. I'll go, because I never approved of actin' like that toward no woman. I'll. . . ."

The range boss spoke up gruffly. "All right. Let's get the hell down there."

IX

They went first to rig out animals for the two fresh captives, then all four of them walked back out where Rufe and Jud had left their animals, and it was there, while they were getting ahorseback, that the range boss, looking skeptically at Rufe, said: "You scairt the whey out of old Abe about the fellers who went over to burn the barn . . . now tell me what really happened over there? You fellers never killed nobody."

Jud said: "Didn't we, then?"

Ruff shook his head. "Mister, on a night like this, no farther off than the Cane place is, if there'd been much gunfire, the sound would have carried."

Jud smiled. "From inside a barn?" He gestured. "Line out your horse and shut up."

They crossed back through the yard of Chase's unkempt cow camp and picked up the wide trail southeastward. There was no talk now, not that Rufe or Jud would have objected, but since they held all the initiative, and they were silent, neither the range boss nor the camp cook spoke up.

Finally they arrived at the pass leading down off the mesa. It became clear why Elisabeth had said no one could come up, or go down, without being intercepted. The trail led straight through Chase's camp, which had clearly been no accident.

The trail was wide and well marked. In fact, it would only take a little work in some fallen-in places to make it fit for wagons again. But since the passing of Elisabeth's parents, no one had maintained the road, so now it was simply a wide, very good saddleback trail.

Heat rose up from down below. The farther down they rode, the more noticeable this was. Apparently summer was already over the desert country.

Jud turned to the cook, who was riding on his left side by Jud's order, and said: "How old are you?"

Smith replied with a succinct answer: "Sixty-six."

Jud gazed placidly at him as he made a vocal judgment. "Hell, you've lived long enough. My pappy didn't make it that far along by seven years."

Abe Smith lacked Pete Ruff's iron obviously. He shot Jud a frantic look. "I didn't do a blessed thing. They never confided in me, and they never asked me for no help."

The range boss, who was riding on Rufe's left side, leaned to speak, and Rufe's arm shot out to jolt him into silence. They exchanged a look, and the range boss eased back in the saddle, furious but silent. Rufe did not know what his partner was leading up to, and he was interested enough not to want any digressions.

Then it became clear what was on Jud's mind. "A man who feeds folks three times a day for a fact hears a lot. Like you told us, old bastard." Jud grinned at Abe Smith. "You've heard 'em talking about running off the lady's horses and cattle, eh?"

Abe squirmed in the saddle, stared flintily dead

ahead, out over the dark desert, then he swung helplessly to glance back. But Pete Ruff was like a hawkish, mahogany statue back there and offered not a sound.

Jud leaned and rapped the old man's leg. "Nobody lives forever, do they . . . old bastard?"

"Men talk," blurted out the anguished old man. "They always got to be talking about something. It don't usually mean much, but. . . ."

Jud lifted out the gun and rested it in his lap, gazing across at the *cocinero*, and finally Pete Ruff came to old Smith's aid.

"Hell, tell 'em," he growled.

Whatever Ruff's reason, it was all the encouragement old Smith needed. He said: "Yeah, I've heard all the talk, only nobody done stole her livestock, mister. They run 'em down off the mesa out over the desert. They was all branded. Chase wouldn't take that kind of a chance, so they just got scattered out all over the desert."

Rufe looked at the range boss and got a bleak nod of confirmation. "That's true. Maybe they got stole down there. I've got no way of knowing because none of us ever went back down looking for 'em. But *we* sure as hell never stole them. The idea was to clean her out."

"It didn't work," stated Rufe.

The range boss shrugged thick, compact shoulders. "So . . . she was to get burned out," he explained, then looked bleakly over at Rufe. "Me, I'd have burned her out first, long ago." He did not look even slightly conscience-stricken as he made this announcement. "It'd be doin' her a favor. It don't make one lick of sense for a single woman owning all that good land up there, trying to run a ranch by herself.

The best thing that could have happened would have been for her to get forced off the mesa and into a house down in town, where single womenfolk had ought to be."

Rufe did not argue, did not speak at all when the range boss had finished his challenging statement. His was a very commonplace range-country conviction, and even Rufe did not entirely disagree with it. A place like Cane's Mesa was *not* settled, fenced, orderly cow country. It was not a place where a lone woman could have managed, but, hell, it wasn't up to men like Chase and his range boss to decide for Elisabeth Cane. It was *her* decision.

They reached the flat country, and it was vastly different from the mesa. The ground was flinty, rain-lashed, covered with an endless variety of spindly, wiry underbrush, most of it bearing sharp thorns, and, if this had been broad daylight instead of small hours of late night—or very early morning—it would also have been hot, riding across the desert.

They had no difficulty keeping to the trail. Down here, it was scored by overgrown but clearly discernible wagon ruts, additional reminders that old Amos Cane had pioneered this country, and, as the trail angled through the brush clumps, a sliver of moonlight arrived unexpectedly, which aroused Jud's interest.

Overhead, those massive, water-laden shapes were breaking up. It could still rain, but apparently a high, savage wind above the clouds was shredding them, forcing them out of their threatening formations, scattering them from the center outward.

It had never smelled like rain to Rufe, but he had refrained from mentioning this to Jud earlier because it was not important. If it had rained, they would have got soaked, and that was about the size of it, but if it did not rain, they would remain dry, which was about the size of that, too.

The hawk-faced half-breed range boss rolled and lit a cigarette, then blew smoke and looked calmly over at Rufe. "You figure to go up against Bull Harris?" he asked with a dry, clinical interest.

Rufe considered his answer a long while before giving it. "Depends on Harris, I expect, and maybe it also depends upon your boss."

Pete Ruff made a little snorting sound. "Arlen won't take you on. He don't have to, mister. Fellers like Arlen Chase *hire* that kind of work done."

Rufe studied Pete Ruff. He knew the type, had worked for them in a dozen different territories. They were top-notch range stockmen, beyond that other considerations such as encroachment, crowding others off a range, expanding their grasslands, and organizing the crews and the cow camps were incidental. They did those things, when it fell to them to become so occupied, with an almost offhand pragmatism. Their first and foremost interest was their herds and enough grass for their herds. They were not entirely unprincipled men; they were products of an environment that was never mild, and they became exactly the same way.

Even Ruff's dispassionate interest in what might occur in Clearwater was consistent with the kind of man he was. Rufe thought privately that it was too bad Elisabeth hadn't got hold of this range boss before Arlen Chase had hired him on. There was no unyielding antagonism between them. They were too much alike for that. What was different was that they happened to be on opposite sides of the fence.

Up ahead, Jud and Abe Smith were quietly talking about the prospects of the law's involvement when they got down to Clearwater. Abe was worried half sick, but Abe was an old man, and that probably made him more susceptible to worry. But Jud did nothing to mitigate the old cook's anxiety for an obvious reason; he wanted Abe Smith to talk his head off in front of the law in Clearwater.

Rufe and Pete Ruff slouched along a few yards back, listening, reading their own interpretations into what Jud and Abe were talking about, and said nothing.

Finally, though, when they came out of the desert and walked their horses up onto an arrow-straight north-south hardpan stage road, the range boss said: "You fellers been lucky up to now. That's all. Chase never figured you'd be as clever as you turned out to be. But you're still a hell of a long way from getting him, and gettin' me 'n' Abe into the Clearwater jailhouse don't amount to much. You boys ain't even begun to face trouble yet."

Rufe was half inclined to agree with this, but he would never have conceded as much to Chase's range boss. All he said in reply was: "Luck sure helps, for a fact, but there's something else just as valuable."

"What?" challenged the range boss.

"Surprise," retorted Rufe, and stood in his stirrups trying to see rooftops downcountry. "Chase don't know us from Adam's off ox." He settled back down. "And neither you, nor old bastard up ahead there, are going to be able to help him."

Ruff said—"The constable'll tell him."—and that brought Jud twisting around to stare bleakly at the range boss. Ruff shrugged. "It's a fact. Arlen Chase is a big pumpkin hereabouts. This is cowman country."

Jud swung forward without saying a word. They continued down the stage road for slightly more than a mile before Rufe wrinkled his nose at the faint fragrance of wood smoke. It was too early for most folks to be firing up their cook stoves for breakfast, so this aroma had to be left over, in the heavy, motionless night air, from the previous evening's supper fires.

Nevertheless, they still did not catch sight of the town for some time afterward, a thin little shaft of moonlight notwithstanding.

A low, warm wind came along from the north, ruffling dust in the roadway and making underbrush sway a little. It smelled dry as old bones to Rufe. He was more confident than ever that it would not rain.

Jud raised an arm. "Town ahead."

Neither of Chase's men commented, and all Rufe did was sit straighter in the saddle to see the rooftops and some dark-etched treetops against the faintly iridescent, paling belly of the roiled heavens.

Ruff smashed out his cigarette atop his saddle horn, black eyes sardonically fixed dead ahead upon Clearwater. He did not have to say what he was thinking; his expression did that for him. He did not believe this was the end of anything; he believed it was the beginning. He also believed that two faded-looking top hands who had been purely lucky up until now were shortly going to learn a lesson about bucking a real scheming cowman.

Jud raised his rein hand and growled for Abe to follow, then veered from the roadway while they were still a half mile or so from the environs of town. Abe started to ask a garrulous question, and Jud glared. Abe subsided. He no longer actually believed Jud was the killer he had formerly thought him to be, but neither did he believe Jud wasn't entirely capable of knocking someone off their saddle.

It was the range boss, scowling as he watched the two riders up ahead leave the stage road, who said: "Where's he going?"

Rufe had no idea, but he and Jud had worked too well, too long as a team for him to worry much, so all he said was: "Wait and see."

It was that statement the range boss had made about Clearwater's town constable being on the side of men like Arlen Chase that had inspired Jud to leave the road with their prisoners. He had no intention of handing Ruff and Smith over to some damned cowman-owned town constable who would then rush forth and raise the alarm.

The land west of Clearwater was marked off by dozens of small acreages where fenced-in patches of land contained everything from goats and sheep, to pigs and milk cows, and harness horses.

There were huge trees in all directions, which mitigated the otherwise harshness of the desert landscape. Actually Clearwater did not really squat on the desert, but rather upon the northernmost, upper edge of it. There was water up there, while only a few miles due southward, there was no water, and no trees. Down there was where New Mexico's arid country began.

X

Rufe and Jud had time on their side, but it was not something indefinite, not with a paleness beginning to show along the undersides of the clouds.

Clearwater was something else. It was not a rough cow town, obviously; there were brick stores and handsome, painted residences, fenced yards, and trees. In daylight it would undoubtedly be a pretty town, but neither Rufe nor Jud were concerned with that. Their problem was that they had never been anywhere near Clearwater before and wanted to find a place to hide their prisoners. It would have solved all their problems if they had been able simply to ride in and turn Smith and Ruff over to the constable, but, as Jud growled to Rufe when they were picking their way around and through the little meandering back roads, their only real advantage was that no one knew yet what had happened on Cane's Mesa. That left the advantage with Elisabeth Cane's faction, and to sacrifice that advantage now, in a town likely to be hostile to strangers, wouldn't be either very wise or, probably, very healthy.

Pete Ruff wore a small, smug smile while the four of them rode aimlessly. It was old Abe Smith who complained a little, from time to time, and, when

Jud finally halted alongside a tumble-down old carriage shed some distance from the nearest other building, Smith said: "I ain't going to make a peep. You can depend on that. I don't want no trouble. At my age all folks want to do is hang on a little longer." He looked at the old shed and wagged his head. "It'll have rats as big as dogs in it, boys."

Jud dismounted and disappeared inside the old building. While he was gone, Pete Ruff started another cigarette, but Rufe told him to throw it away. They did not need a lighted torch to alert any possible wakening townsmen. Ruff obeyed, then smiled more broadly as Jud returned, knocking dust and cobwebs off himself. "There ain't a place around here you can hide us," Ruff said.

Jud came over, looked at Ruff, and also smiled. Without explaining the smile, he gestured for the prisoners to dismount. He was still smiling when he drew his gun to herd them into the old carriage house. Rufe kept watch and said nothing, but once they were inside, the weak, ghostly light filtering through the sagging, ancient roof showed a large, earthen-floored, trash-littered vacant space. Rufe wrinkled his nose; there was a strong smell of sour mash inside the old building.

Jud herded his captives to the center of the room, then ordered them to halt, stepped around in front, heaved mightily, and a dusted-over, heavy wooden trap door came up, for the second time. Earlier Jud had almost fallen, when he'd snagged a boot toe in the ring latch.

Pete Ruff stopped smiling and leaned to look straight down. Abe Smith made a slight strangling sound in his throat. Rufe came forward also to look down. This was where that smell of sour mash was coming from. Someone, at one time, had manufactured whiskey down in that hole.

Jud dropped a match to see how deep the dugout was. Then, satisfied, he told Pete Ruff to climb down in there. Ruff turned in quick, hard hostility and Jud cocked his Colt.

Ruff went to the edge, shoved his legs over, peered down, reversed himself, gripping the edge, and let his body hang to its full limit, then let go. The hole was about ten or twelve feet deep, and as dark inside as any such hole would have been. Pete Ruff landed hard, and cursed as he got painfully up to his feet. They could see his lifted face.

Abe Smith bitterly complained. He even asked for one of the lariats off a saddle outside. Jud gruffly ordered him to descend as Ruff had done, and, although old Abe cried out that his bones were too brittle, that he was an old, helpless, innocent, completely uninvolved individual, he nonetheless sat upon the edge exactly as the range boss had previously done, groaning all the while, swung around, and dropped down. His landing was perfect; in fact, although he almost fell, he managed not to by bumping into Ruff. Then he looked up piteously.

"Don't close the lid," he pleaded. "I told you . . . I won't try to rouse nobody, only don't close the damned lid. A feller could suffercate down in here."

Jud leaned to lift the lid. As he raised it, he ignored Smith and spoke directly to the range boss: "You start hollering and raise the town, mister, and you'll trade this hole for another one around here somewhere . . . wherever their graveyard is. You've done your part . . . now keep out of it until we come back for you."

He lowered the lid with Abe Smith's quavering

lamentations becoming muted to whisper strength through the heavy wooden cover.

Jud looked over at Rufe. "Someone's sure on our side tonight."

Rufe's reply was neutral about that. "How did you find it?"

"Damned near broke my foot catching it in the ring." Jud led the way back to the horses. They led the AC animals quietly down a back alley until they came to the public corrals, off-saddled them, turned them in, flung the saddlery in some shadows where it would probably not be found and stolen, then they went in search of some hay. This proved easier to find than Jud's bootleg whiskey hole. There were several loose stacks out back of a livery barn. They helped themselves, forked feed to the AC animals, then took their own horses around to the main roadway, climbed aboard, and casually rode on down to where a pair of lanterns hanging outside a whitewashed log building indicated the location of Clearwater's livery barn.

There was supposed to be a night man around, but they did not find him even though they looked in the harness room, the feed room, even a little office scented with horse sweat.

In the end, they cared for their own animals, and by then the paleness over against the eastern rims was steadily widening along toward sunrise. It would still be another hour or so before the sun actually appeared, but now that scent they had detected earlier, of cook stove coals, was beginning to get stronger, which meant that the housewives of Clearwater were firing up to cook breakfast.

They walked back out front, and nearly fell over a small, wiry old man who was coming sleepily in from where he had been sleeping in a hay wagon. He was rubbing his eyes and did not see either Rufe or Jud until they side-stepped to avoid the collision. Then he dropped his fists and blinked in surprise.

Rufe grinned at him. "You need some coffee, partner," he said, and the startled night man agreed with a big yawn, followed by a strong nod of his head.

"Sure do. How come you fellers up so blasted early?"

"Light sleepers," stated Rufe. "You the nighthawk?"

"Yeah," mumbled the small, sinewy, elfin-like hostler. "Come on down to the harness room and I'll fire up the stove for coffee." He looked around. "Where'd you leave your animals?"

"Already stalled and fed," replied Rufe, turning with Jud to follow the older man. They needed information about Clearwater and, next to a bartender, the best source in any town was either a liveryman or one of his hostlers.

The livery barn hostler's repeated yawnings inspired a reaction in Jud. Before they entered the harness room, he had yawned three times.

The night man kept up a running fire of mumbled conversation as he lit a lamp, hung it from an overhead nail, then shaved kindling into a small cast-iron stove, and, when he had that appliance crackling, busied himself with making a fresh pot of coffee.

He really did not require answers to most of his questions. Nor did he usually wait for an answer before going on to the next question, or on a tangent of robust swearing at either the coffee pot or the stove.

When he finally turned, though, everything ordered the way he felt that it should be, his small, keen eyes made a steady study of the larger, younger men. They looked exactly like what he thought they were—commonplace range riders. There was no reason for them to look otherwise, that is exactly what they were—except, perhaps, to the folks back in the Gila Valley, and also except to some men chained up in Elisabeth Cane's log barn, and down in someone's old bootleg whiskey hide-out, much nearer than the Cane log barn.

Jud offered openers by saying Clearwater appeared to be a fine town. The hostler pursed his lips, pinched down his eyes, and heavily pondered for a moment before replying to the effect that, yes, Clearwater was a good enough place to live, but it had its drawbacks.

Jud thought all towns had drawbacks, which the hostler assented was highly probable, although, since he'd been raised in Kansas during the troubles, and had afterward spent most of his life on the south desert, or as far north as Denver, but no farther, he really could not make a sweeping judgment about *all* towns.

Jud smiled. Every town had at least one—men like this, usually undersize, coarse-featured, in this man's case goat-eyed, meaning one blue eye, one green or brown eye, very ignorant and ungrammatical, but convinced they were very clever and knowledgeable.

There was one advantage. These people equated knowing other folks' business, with being intelligent. If they could discourse loftily on the affairs of others, making purest gossip out of it, they thought that amounted to being intelligent. Rufe and Jud knew this hostler's type of individual, and, without having really to exert much effort, they coaxed him to discussing his fellow citizens. The town constable, for example, a rather large man, in his prime, whose name was Homer Bradshaw, and of whom his enemies said he had been a much better blacksmith than he was now a peace officer.

The nighthawk repeated that tale, to make Jud and Rufe smile. They dutifully smiled. He then mentioned some of the personal facts about Homer Bradshaw, ending up with a comment Jud and Rufe remembered. He said: "Him and a couple other fellers been pickin' up cattle off the desert the past year, and doin' right well with 'em. Seems they're strays that been wanderin' loose ever since Indians wiped out a train of settlers six, eight years back. Of course, that's plumb legal, but folks been complainin' a little that Homer's spent more time out of town than in town this past year, and they don't like payin' his wages if he ain't around to earn 'em."

Rufe, taking his cue from the way the hostler recounted his story, sympathized with the irate townsmen, saying: "That's plumb right. Folks need protection, not some lawman who's tryin' to get rich instead of minding his business. Incidentally, where does Homer peddle these strays he catches?"

The hostler was unsure. "Mexico, I think, but maybe not, because that's a far drive southward. I don't rightly know."

"Are they branded animals?"

"Oh, yeah!" exclaimed the hostler. "I only seen a couple of the horses . . . saddle stock it was. The brand was sort of blurry, and they was across a corral from me. I couldn't make it out. Homer don't corral his gather in the holding pens below town." The hostler grinned about this. "I wouldn't, neither, in his boots, with folks half mad at me for catching them strays. I think he drives 'em south, down into the desert somewhere. Maybe he delivers 'em to buyers down there."

The hostler slid to his feet and went to the stove where the coffee was finally boiling merrily away, and outside in the barn's chilly runway that corpse-gray predawn light was turning gradually toward a blushing, soft shade of pink.

Rufe rolled a cigarette, lit it, and ran a thoughtful hand over his beard-stubbled face. When the hostler finally filled three cups of not-bad java, Rufe asked him a question.

"Is Homer a friend of a cowman named Arlen Chase?"

The night man slyly winked. "You want to know what I figure . . . in secret, of course? I figure it was Mister Chase told Homer about them strays."

Rufe affected surprise. "No! Why would Mister Chase do that?"

"Dunno," stated the hostler, "but I can tell you this much. Them critters come off the north and east ranges below Cane's Mesa, and the only cowman up in that country is Mister Chase. He knows every damned animal that's abroad up there. You can bet your hat Mister Chase seen them strays."

"Well, hell," interjected Jud skeptically, "why wouldn't he take them for himself?"

The hostler laughed down his nose at Jud. "Mister Chase, cowboy, is a mighty powerful feller. He don't need no one's ownerless strays. Not by a damned sight. Mister Chase is a feller everyone hereabouts respects all to hell."

Rufe drank his coffee, looked out to watch dawn arrive, then thanked the hostler for his coffee and his interesting conversation, and was ready to move forth into the new day. He only had one more question.

"What's the name of one of those fellers who work the strays with Homer?"

"Matthew Reilly," replied the hostler. "Sure you boys wouldn't want another cup? This here's the best java I ever made."

XI

The café man was watering down the roadway out front of his establishment when Rufe and Jud ambled up. He flung the water, twisting his body as he did this, so that the bucket load would be sent forth in a high arch and cover more ground. Then he turned back and, seeing two faded range men watching, said: "You'd be surprised how many damned people in this world don't have any more manners'n lope up a dusty road through the center of town in summertime. Well, come on in, fellers . . . I got something for breakfast you damned seldom get any more. Antelope steaks. Set there at the counter while I rassle it up. I'll be back with the coffee directly."

They sat at the counter, looked back out into the chilly, faint-lighted dawn roadway, saw a few indications that Clearwater was coming to life, then faced forward as their coffee arrived. Rufe let the cup sit there, but Jud had no objection to this café man's coffee atop the hostler's coffee. Jud rolled a smoke as he slouched at the counter with his coffee.

"We better find Matthew Reilly," he murmured.

Rufe sighed. "I expect so. But, hell, we're not down here to clean up Clearwater."

Jud conceded that. "True enough. How else can

we get anyone locked up? If their town constable is runnin' off Elisabeth's livestock, then he's hand-in-glove with Arlen Chase, and we can't do a damned thing about Chase until we take care of their damned town marshal, can we?"

Rufe sighed again. This was precisely what he had been thinking when he'd first sighed, and he did not like the implications. So far, they'd had a lot of luck. So far, too, they'd had their special advantage—no one knew who they were or what they were up to—but taking on a town constable in his own town with them being total strangers. . . .

The café man brought their breakfasts, and, as a stocky, sleepy-looking range man walked in out of the cold roadway, the café man glanced up, then said: " 'Morning, Matthew. Set down. I'll fetch your breakfast in a minute."

Rufe and Jud raised their eyes. Matthew was a young man, powerfully put together, sandy-headed and gray-eyed. He went to the bench and eased down, scratched himself, then yawned mightily.

The name was common enough, and, except for the fact that this particular Matthew fit the description of a range man, Rufe and Jud might not have been interested. As it was, they ate slowly and in silence, and had a second cup of java, and even smoked afterward to pass time until Matthew was finished. As he arose to count out coins, Rufe and Jud did the same. They then followed Matthew out into the roadway, which had a few pedestrians here and there, men heading for their jobs around town, merchants getting ready for the new day, and, as Matthew paused to resettle the hat atop his head, Rufe and Jud stepped up on each side casually, as though they were all old friends, and asked what his last name was.

The stocky man looked from Rufe to Jud before answering. "Reilly. Matt Reilly. Who are you fellers?"

Jud pointed to a wall bench up the plank walk out front of a shop. "Walk up there and set, Matt. We're just a couple of fellers that'd like a few words with you."

Matthew Reilly was puzzled. He completed the resettling of his hat, looked closer at Rufe and Jud, then slowly reddened.

Jud smiled. "You don't want to go and do something foolish, Matt." Jud kept smiling from a distance of perhaps four or five feet. "Walk up to that god-damned bench, Matt!"

Reilly walked. Once, when a stalwart man with a sprinkling of gray over the ears, threw Reilly a casual wave as he hastened southward on the opposite side of the roadway, Matt half-heartedly raised a hand to return the salute. Because Reilly seemed about to hail that man over here, who had a dully-glowing badge upon his vest front, Jud tapped him lightly on the back.

"Just walk, and keep quiet," he said.

They got to the bench. Reilly sank down with a stranger still on each side, flanking him, and with both big hands upon his knees he looked from Jud to Rufe. "What the hell is this all about?"

Rufe wasted no time. "Who've you been selling those Cane cattle and horses to, Matt?"

The stocky man stared steadily at Rufe for a long time before answering. "Just who the hell are you, anyway?" he demanded.

Jud spoke, from Matt's left side. "You answer,

Matt, you don't ask. If you want trouble, you've got it all around you by the ton. You figure it'd bother us to kill you right here in the middle of the road of your town this morning?"

Rufe asked the question again. "Who've you been selling those Lance-and-Shield critters to, Matt?"

The stocky man leaned, staring hard at the scuffed duckboards at his feet. "I sell *strays* to anyone wants to buy 'em."

"Lance-and-shield are Cane critters," said Rufe, "and you know it. So does Arlen Chase know it. So does the damned law you just waved to across the road know it. Isn't that right, Matt?"

Reilly raised his face, peering across the road and slightly southward where the man with the badge had disappeared inside a handsome brick building that had close-set steel bars in front of the roadside windows.

"Matt . . . ?"

Reilly turned toward Rufe again. He formed words with his lips but did not utter them. Rufe stared unwaveringly. "I'm not famous for bein' a patient man," he murmured. "And I haven't had my man for breakfast yet this morning. Matt, I'm sure beginnin' to take a powerful dislike to you."

Reilly finally spoke. "Chase knew. What the hell . . . it was him run them Cane critters down off the mesa onto the desert. Chase and his men knew."

"And Homer Bradshaw?"

Reilly licked his lips and continued to stare at Rufe. He was armed, but the man sitting there on his right was as close to his six-gun as he was. Reilly was no coward, but neither was he a simpleton, and that is what it would have taken for a man to try something violent against the two relaxed, bronzed range men sitting here with Reilly. The longer Matt Reilly sat with those two strangers, the more it seemed to him that they *would* kill him.

"Yeah, Homer knew," he admitted finally. "In fact, it's been Homer's deal. I just sort of shared in it with him a little."

"Who else shared in it with you boys?" asked Rufe.

"Feller named Ed Dunway, but he left us last winter, taken his share and went back to Texas. Since then it's been just Homer and me."

Rufe raised an arm to the back of the bench and turned slightly so that he could see past to where Jud was sitting. Jud had been listening, but he had also been studying the handsome brick jailhouse. Now, with unlighted brown-paper cigarette drooping from his mouth, Jud said: "I figure we've just about got to take over that jailhouse, Rufe. We got 'em chained, or buried, or something, all over the damned countryside, and we just might forget where we got some of 'em cached. If we had that jailhouse, it'd sure make things a sight easier, wouldn't you think?"

Rufe considered the building with a very tall old tree out front and to one side of the cribbed old tie rack. "Homer still in there?" he softly asked.

Jud nodded. "Yup. Been watching for him to come out." Jud arose and hoisted his britches as he looked down at Reilly. "Matt, you just sort of lead the way right on in over there, and mind your manners because we're going to be one step behind you."

Rufe also arose. The last man to stand up was Matthew Reilly. He looked very worried as he stepped from beneath the wooden overhead awning out into the roadway, trooping on an angling course in the direction of the jailhouse. He slackened pace as he stepped up over there, then turned and with a twisted look on his face said: "Listen fellers, Homer ain't going to just be walked in on. You can't take him like you taken me in front of the café."

Jud was unimpressed by the warning. With a hand lying upon his pistol butt he said: "You'll be in front, Matt. You better hope to God he don't get bronco, or you're going to look like a miner's sluice box . . . from him and from us." Jud nodded. "Go on. Walk in and be god-damned careful."

Matt crossed to the door, took down a big breath, seized the latch, squeezed, shoved open the door, and stepped inside. The constable was behind his desk looking at a paper when he saw his caller, and boomed out a rough greeting. "How the hell are you this morning, Matt? I figured you'd be sleeping in."

Rufe and Jud stepped in, slightly behind Matt and one on each side, guns fisted and aimed. Constable Bradshaw was stunned, but that passed in moments. He started to swell in the neck and redden in the face. He looked furiously at Matt Reilly.

"What the tarnation hell do you think you're doing?" he roared.

Reilly answered truthfully. "I don't know who they are either, Homer. They caught me outside the café. They been asking about the Cane cattle and horses."

The moment Reilly got that last sentence out, Constable Bradshaw's eyes sprang wide and his head shot up. He did not have to announce what he had just realized—that the two, faded, bronzed, capable-looking men with guns in their fists staring at him, were the two men Arlen Chase had told him about last night at the saloon. Elisabeth Cane's new riders.

Jud said: "Tell you what, Constable. You stand just like that. Don't you so much as take down a big breath, and you'll live to tell your grandchildren about the time you got locked up in your own jail-house."

Jud moved around, staying well out of reach, then he came in behind the lawman, and reached very carefully to lift away Bradshaw's holstered Colt. He backed clear the same way, keeping out of the law-man's reach.

None of them relaxed until after this had hap-pened. Jud shoved the extra six-gun into his waist-band, disarmed Matthew Reilly as well, then smiled at Rufe.

The ring of cell keys was atop the desk. Rufe used these to open the cell room door and, farther along, also to open the strap-steel doors of adjoining cells. Jud pushed their prisoners inside so Rufe could lock them in. Then Jud, holstering his weapon, said: "Where is Arlen Chase, Constable?"

Bradshaw stood in the center of his little cage, legs wide, hands on hips, glaring without saying a word.

Rufe finished with the locking and did not holster his weapon; he handed it to Jud, instead, then asked the same question. "Constable, Chase came to town last night with his gunfighter. Where are they?"

This time there was an answer, but the clear menace of Rufe's handing aside his gun as though he would enter the cell and beat the answer out of Homer Brad-shaw did not seem to be the reason for Bradshaw's re-ply. He smiled when he gave it. He was thinking of Bull Harris, no doubt, and the outcome when these two range riders went up against the professional gunfighter.

"Arlen keeps a room at the boarding house east of town, around the corner from the drayage company's yard. But about now I'd say he's likely either havin' breakfast at the café, or maybe he's having an eye-opener at the saloon."

Homer Bradshaw continued to smile savagely as he looked from Rufe to Jud. The man in the adjoining cell, though, did not smile. In fact, Matt Reilly looked dubious, and he had to understand the reason behind his friend's smile. He also had reason to look doubtful concerning a meeting between Chase and Harris and these two strangers. The strangers had a knack for just materializing out of nowhere on either side of a man, and, if they could do that, Reilly had a strong notion they would know a few other tricks as well.

"Just set," ordered Jud. "Don't start hollering or rattling the doors, because if we got to come back for you . . . hell, it'll be like shooting at fish in a rain barrel, won't it?"

They returned to the front office where Rufe tossed down the gun he had taken from the lawman. There were now a pair of Colts atop the constable's desk. He turned to Jud with a suggestion. "Suppose we go fetch Smith and Ruff down here, too."

Rufe was not thinking about the welfare of the pair of men in the bootleg hole; he was trying to think of a way to separate Chase from his gunfighter. The idea of going up against Arlen Chase, who was no better than Rufe or Jud probably, because he, too, was a cowman, caused Rufe no particular anxiety. But going up against Bull Harris, the professional, was altogether different, and facing them both did not appeal to Rufe at all.

"They can stay in the damned hole," Jud growled,

and went to a barred window to lean, looking up the roadway in the direction of the café and the saloon.

Rufe said: "We got to cut Chase out and get him by himself. Otherwise, the odds aren't too good."

"Easy," replied Jud, so nonchalantly that Rufe began scowling. "I'll amble around until I find them, then I'll get Chase aside and ask him for work. He don't know me from General Grant. While I got him to one side, you can have Bull Harris. How's that sound?"

Rufe continued to scowl. "How's it sound? Like you're trying to get me killed, that's how it sounds."

Jud considered. "Yeah, it does sound a mite like that, don't it? You ready?"

"Hell, no."

Jud nodded. "Fine. Then let's go."

They walked out of the jailhouse together, locked the door after themselves, and paused a moment in the golden, warm sunshine.

XII

The café man shook his head. He hadn't seen Mister Chase since the evening before at suppertime, and that black-bearded, mean-looking feller with Mister Chase hadn't been around this morning, either. Maybe, the café man suggested, they were having breakfast at the saloon. There was a corner of the bar where folks who bought drinks up there could slice up some meat and bread and make sandwiches.

The sun was rising a foot at a time, rather than inches, the way it always seemed to do on the summertime desert. It had not yet crested above the roof peaks of the town, but it was getting close, and the lower-down shadows were getting paler and were also retreating.

The battered wagon of some cow outfit appeared in the roadway at the lower end of town, scuffing runnels of tawny dust from beneath its steel tires. Otherwise, excluding a pair of horsemen entering from the opposite end of town, up where Rufe and Jud had entered last night—or early this morning—there was only walking traffic so far. But it was early yet.

Across the road, the jailhouse was still partially in cool shadows. It was also quiet, and no one was around to try the locked door, which was perhaps just as well. Rufe said: "I don't know how much time we got, Jud, but it can't be a hell of a lot."

They started in the direction of the saloon. From far off, and up along the slope of Cane's Mesa's easternmost side, a quick, blinding flash of intense white light appeared and was gone. Jud saw it at the same time Rufe caught the same reflection. They stopped, peering off miles northwesterly.

"Someone coming down off the mesa," stated Jud. "Maybe those fellers in Elisabeth's barn got loose somehow."

Rufe nodded. That was possible, but it did not really interest him very much. What did interest him was the clear fact that their advantage was finally running out. Whoever that was coming down off the mesa would surely be heading for town. And even if it took them a couple of hours or more to get here, those two men in a bootleg hole weren't going to stay down there forever, either.

Rufe said: "Let's get this over with before we got a whole countryside jumpin' down our gullets."

They went to the saloon, and Jud entered first, leaving Rufe ostensibly loitering outside, watching the roadway. Not because he felt it needed watching—not yet anyway—but because, if Chase were in there and he could be braced about a riding job, the chances of one man being hired was a lot better than two men being hired.

A pair of slouching cowboys passed Rufe, looked over, and nodded. Rufe nodded back. The man with the battered cow-camp wagon was turning down into a narrow little roadway south of the general store. No one had to tell Rufe where he was going. To the rear loading dock of the store for sacks of flour, sugar, pinto beans, most likely, and tins of molasses.

A graying, slightly stooped older man, thin as a rail and with a perpetually saturnine expression, hauled up out front of the saloon's inviting doors and looked in over their tops, then he grunted when he saw Rufe, and said: "I'm the doctor. I look in every morning to see which of the damned alcoholics 'round town are backsliding." He turned to squint out into the sun-brightening roadway. "You an early morning drinker, by any chance, young man?"

Rufe grinned. "Nope. I'm not even a very good nighttime drinker, Doctor."

The old man grunted again. "Good. Stay that way, and you'll keep your liver. Bad enough, being in the saddle most of your life, young man. Most cowboys, by the time they're my age, got a bunk-wetting problem. That's bad enough . . . but heading for a damned saloon every time they hit town compounds it. A man's not one damned bit better'n his liver, young man. You remember that, eh?"

Rufe said—"I'll remember it."—and amusedly watched the gaunt old stooped man go walking stiffly southward down in the direction of the general store.

A wispy, elfin figure was hurrying northward, in the direction of the saloon's doors, head down, features pinched in concentration. At the very last minute the elfin man looked up, and saw the medical practitioner bearing down and whisked so swiftly into a store-front doorway that Rufe marveled. He had recognized the elfin man as the livery barn nighthawk. Apparently he was one of the early morning drinkers the doctor had been seeking.

After the doctor had marched past, looking neither right nor left, the hostler peeked out, made certain the doctor was far down toward the general store, stepped forth, and hurriedly came on.

Rufe pretended to be looking the other way when the elfin older man turned and disappeared beyond the spindle doors. Moments later Jud ambled out, lighted cigarette trailing smoke, his eyes narrowed in thought, and said: "They got surprisingly good beer in there. You should have come in and had one."

Rufe frowned. "Where's Chase?"

"Not there. Neither is the gunfighter. But the barman told me they're due any minute." Jud's eyes lifted to the faraway tawny barranca where they had seen that flash of brilliant light of someone's silver cheek piece or *concha*. "What's botherin' me, Rufe, is that maybe they took off from town, heading back for the cow camp."

Rufe also turned to gaze out across the flat country in the direction of Cane's Mesa. If Jud's worry was valid, then there was going to be some serious trouble, because, sure as hell, when Chase got to his camp and found it empty, he was going to ride for the Cane place—with his gunfighter.

"Luck might be runnin' out," muttered Jud, and spat out the cigarette. He rallied then, and said: "You take the yonder side of the road, I'll take this side, and by God we'd better find those two fellers by the time we get down by the livery barn, or, sure as hell they'll be on their way back, and we'll have to go hightailing it after them."

Rufe shoved off the log wall and, without speaking, ambled out into the morning warmth bound across the dusty roadway.

From now on, they could not afford to be secretive and clever; they had to make their determination about Chase and his man killer the quickest way possible, and that meant they might also come up against exactly what Rufe did not want them to come up against—a head-on meeting, two for two. He was not a professional gunman and neither was Jud. They were fast, and they were also accurate with handguns, but they were no better than most range men, which meant they were not in the same class Bull Harris was in.

Rufe's side of the road had about a dozen business establishments, and most of them had front windows allowing someone outside to look the length and breadth of the inside counters and shelves. One place, the harness and saddle works, had that same kind of a big window, but it had been so cluttered with heavy sets of leather and chain harness, fine driving harness, saddlery, boots, bridles, and odds and ends that it was impossible to see through.

Ruff stepped back to the doorway and sauntered into an atmosphere wonderfully fragrant of leather and harness oil and pipe smoke. The bald, grizzled man in the canvas apron at the cutting table peered over the tops of his steel-rimmed eyeglasses, puffed smoke a moment, then removed the stubby pipe to say: "Welcome, *amigo*. Don't just stand there, come right on in. Don't make a damn whether you buy anything or not." The old man's shrewd, light blue eyes studied Rufe thoughtfully, then made a common enough misjudgment. "There's work to be had around the Clearwater country, and some of the outfits stick notices on the wall in here . . . except that there ain't none stuck on the wall today. But if you care to set and talk a little, maybe someone'll come in looking for a rider, and you'll get hired on."

Rufe went over and leaned upon the counter,

looking at the harness maker. "I'm hunting for a man named Arlen Chase," he said.

The old man's face showed the faintest of very fleeting shadows of disapproval, but if Rufe hadn't been looking squarely at the old man, he wouldn't have seen it come and go.

"He don't come in here much," stated the saddle maker, wiping palms upon the canvas apron and looking down at the flat-out half hide of skirting leather atop his cutting table.

"But you know him?" asked Rufe, watching closely.

This time the shadow came and went more slowly. The old man was hostile to the name of Arlen Chase, no question about it.

"Yes, I know him. Known Mister Chase many years. Knew him when he first elbowed his way in atop Cane's Mesa." The pale eyes glinted behind the shiny glasses. "And I can tell you, son, if old Amos Cane was still above ground, he'd have Arlen Chase for breakfast, and afterward pick his teeth with Mister Chase's buckle tongue."

Rufe smiled. "I believe you. I'm not looking for him for a job. I just want to find Chase, and right quick."

The old man reached and slowly dragged off his glasses, staring steadily. Finally he softly inclined his head. "All right, mister. All right. I seen Mister Chase and some bushy-faced, ornery-lookin' cuss go into the abstract office down the road below the general store a couple of doors about fifteen minutes ago."

Rufe nodded. "Thanks." He turned and walked out into the roadway, looking southward across the road, and saw Jud just entering the general store.

There was more traffic now, both in the roadway and along both plank walks. In fact, Rufe was delayed in reaching the general store because of the traffic. Over across the road a heavy-set, raffish-looking man was rattling the jailhouse front doorway. Rufe saw this, and also saw the stranger turn away with a curse and go stamping along in the direction of the livery barn.

Rufe entered the general store, looked over the heads of half a dozen browsing women until he caught sight of his partner, then worked his way along as far as the steel goods section where Jud had just finished speaking with a man wearing alpaca sleeve protectors up to his elbows. As the store-keeper walked briskly in pursuit of a customer, Jud saw Rufe coming, and relaxed against a pistol case, shoved back his hat, and looked forlorn.

"They're not in town," he said before Rufe had stopped moving. "Nobody's seen 'em. Sure as hell they've headed back to the mesa."

Rufe gestured. "Down a couple of doors . . . in the abstract office."

Jud straightened up without a word and followed his partner back out into the bustling roadway. Southward, the first shop was a bakery; the second store front had gold letters arched across a window which announced that it was the **Abstract Office.**

Jud studied the window, the lettering upon it, the front door, which was closed, then looked quizzically at Rufe. "You sure they're inside?"

"The harness maker saw them enter," Rufe explained, and pointed. "I'll go stand down there, south of the place, and, when they come out, you try to get him to hire you on . . . and cut him loose from Harris like we figured."

Jud nodded, hitched at his trousers, waited until Rufe was down the walkway a short distance where he would be in a position to flank Harris and Chase if shooting erupted, then Jud stepped up close to the bakery's front and started rolling a smoke.

People came and went, and so did the time. Jud had his cigarette half smoked, ready to drop and trample underfoot, before the door of the abstract office opened. He held his cigarette poised to drop, watching intently. A tall, raw-boned, granite-jawed woman with iron-gray hair and a choker-type neckline to her white blouse stepped out and closed the door, looked up and down the plank walk as though she were seeking a challenge, then she turned northward and, with her formidable jaw tilted like the bow of a battleship, marched past Jud without looking at him, and kept right on marching.

Rufe glanced into the busy roadway, glanced at the sun, which was coming close to the rooftops finally, and eventually looked up where Jud was standing—and got a high shrug from his partner, which indicated that Jud was willing to wait a bit longer, but which also indicated he thought they were wasting more time.

Rufe was beginning to think this was so when the office door opened again. This time five men walked out. Bull Harris was identifiable by his black beard and the way he was dressed and wore his ivory-stocked Colt. Arlen Chase was also identifiable because one of the other men, older, heavy-set, wearing a vest and holding a pen in one hand, was very earnestly speaking, using Chase's name now and then. But the other men were completely unexpected. It had not crossed either Jud's or Rufe's mind that Chase and Harris would not come out together, just the pair of them.

Jud leaned and watched, and did not make any move at all when Chase and Harris, along with two of the other men, broke off the discussion in the doorway, and started walking northward, like the woman, without looking left and right.

Bull Harris was silent. Arlen Chase was also silent, most of the time, but the pair of men with him were leaning and talking, one on each side of Arlen Chase, as though their lives depended upon explaining something to him.

The cavalcade passed; Jud glanced down at Rufe with an ironic little smile, and the partners strolled to a meeting out front of the abstract office where they stood and watched Chase and Harris head for the saloon, still with those other two men flanking them.

XIII

The sun was now over the eastern rooftops of Clearwater. The few remaining, diluted shadows vanished in a twinkling. Those heavy clouds that had been overhead the afternoon and night before were distantly visible here and there, torn to shreds by the high wind that had ripped them apart the previous night. The last threat of rainfall was gone.

Rufe, studying the saloon in the midday sun, was not aware of the heavens at all. Neither was Jud, who had a hunch about those two men who had accompanied Chase and Harris to the saloon from the abstract office.

"Land peddlers, or maybe they got a ranch they're trying to work off on him."

The purpose of those men did not interest Rufe. His concern had to do with how much longer they would be at the bar with Arlen Chase. He said—"Hell."—in deep disgust, and straightened up. "Let's go get a beer."

They went up to the saloon, entered, found about a dozen or fifteen other men already lined up for a noonday drink or two, and took a position at the lower end of the bar, watching the men at the upper end, which included Chase and Bull Harris.

The gunfighter acted bored. He had a thick sandwich in one hand and a tall, sticky glass of amber
beer in front of him atop the bar. He was looking out
over the room. His piercing, sweeping glance
reached down as far as the lowest end of the bar,
paused only momentarily upon a pair of faded cowboys down there, who looked as run-of-the-mill as it
was possible for range riders to look, and swept
elsewhere.

Eventually Chase turned upon the pair of fast-
talking men and spoke tersely. Afterward, the two
strangers pulled away from the bar, exchanged a few
more words with Chase, then departed.

Rufe sighed and nudged his partner. Jud let the
strangers get completely out of the saloon before he
stepped back and started up the room.

Rufe made some hard calculations. Jud would
have to get Chase outside, out into the roadway,
without Harris trailing along, before anything could
be accomplished.

But Rufe decided Harris would probably drift
right along with them, and with a firm conviction
that he was not going to allow this to happen, if he
could possibly prevent it, he picked up his beer glass
and also shuffled up in the direction of the upper
end of the bar, except that he turned in midway, just
below the food dishes, and leaned there.

Jud made his approach casually. Rufe saw Chase
look around as Jud addressed him. Harris, too,
looked around, but Harris had already made his assessment of Jud, the worn-looking, down-and-out
range rider, and Harris turned back to the bar to hoist
his beer glass and drink.

Chase listened to Jud. Rufe saw the cowman's
harsh brutish profile relax as he listened, the heavy

mouth begin to tilt slightly with condescension, with scorn, and finally Chase gave a short answer to Jud, and Rufe's partner smiled. Evidently the cowman had either agreed to hire Jud, or offered that kind of encouragement. Jud then spoke again, and this time Chase finished his drink, and turned away from the bar—and Rufe held his breath.

Chase was going to walk out of the saloon with Jud. Harris looked around, eyed the pair of men a moment, then turned back to finish his beer. Rufe's right hand sank gently down to his hip holster. He braced himself to keep Harris inside—then the gunfighter casually reached for another pair of bread slices and went to work making another sandwich, while Chase and Jud crossed the room.

It was going to work!

Rufe forced himself to turn very gradually, very indifferently, to watch the pair of men heading for the door.

Outside, someone let off a high yelp. Several other loud voices suddenly erupted too. Rufe could feel perspiration popping out beneath his shirt. Bull Harris, half-made sandwich in one hand, twisted to look toward the door. So did just about everyone else inside the saloon.

Arlen Chase took two swift strides, grabbed the doors, and shoved through, then stopped dead in his tracks. Rufe could not see much past the cowman's frame, but he saw enough. Several excited men were leading a pair of filthy, limping, utterly bedraggled men down the center of the roadway. Rufe recognized them both. Ruff and Abe Smith!

Rufe felt like swearing. Evidently Jud had recognized the rescued prisoners from the bootleg hole, too, because, without warning, he suddenly reached and gave Arlen Chase a violent punch, knocking him out through the doors and into the roadway.

Rufe was turning when he saw Bull Harris drop his sandwich and suddenly whip around to lunge clear of the bar to face Jud. Rufe stepped away and called.

"Harris!"

The gunfighter whirled, struck instantly by the menace in that shout. Somewhat southward, behind Rufe, two quick-thinking men, lunging frantically to be out of the line of Harris's fire, knocked over two chairs and a table.

Harris was reaching for his gun as he whirled on Rufe. No one could fault Bull Harris's draw. Rufe was already drawing when he shouted, and, although his Colt was clear of leather and tilting into position, the gunfighter's weapon was coming around to bear even faster—then Harris's Colt with its shiny ivory handle slipped in his palm, just as Rufe fired.

Bull Harris was knocked half around by solid impact. He fell against an iron stove, knocking it away from the stovepipe. Soot billowed around as the gunfighter went down and rolled half under a card table.

The sudden silence was deafening.

Throughout the barroom men were frozen in position, staring, most of them with no inkling anything at all was wrong until Rufe's gun went off. Even the barman, who had been alerted by Rufe's shout, hadn't had time to reach for the scatter-gun beneath his countertop, and now it was too late.

Rufe stepped sideways to be well clear of the bar, and faced half around so he could keep most of the patrons, and the bartender, in sight. Not one of them moved a hand, least of all the barman.

An old man, wearing a long coat despite the rising

summer heat, shuffled ahead from shadows along the back wall, and leaned down, staring at Bull Harris. He looked like the Grim Reaper himself, until he put down a hand to touch the ivory-stocked Colt of the dead gunfighter, then he raised up, rubbing his fingers together and said: "Butter. By God he had butter on his fingers. It's all over the handle of his gun."

That, then, accounted for Harris's fatal slip when he was swinging his weapon to bear on Rufe.

No one said a word, but they all watched the old man pick up Harris's six-gun by the barrel, amble to the bar, and drop it there "Look for yourselves," he cackled. "Butter, by God!"

From the roadway men were shouting, and Rufe used the small distraction along the bar to hurry outside. There was no sign of either Arlen Chase or Jud, but a lot of men were heading for the saloon to see what that gunshot had been about. Even the men who had found Pete Ruff and Abe Smith in the old shed were deserting their rescued men to hasten forward.

Rufe headed out through the throng, grabbed Ruff's arm, swore at old Smith, and aimed them in the direction of the jailhouse at a gun-prodded run, expecting any minute for someone to bounce forth from the saloon, yelling for townsmen to stop that man with the gun in his hand.

It did not happen, but, when Rufe was unlocking the jailhouse, a lanky range rider walked out of the saloon and stood there, looking left and right, until he saw Rufe shove the two men into the jailhouse, then the cowboy watched, still without opening his mouth, until Rufe also went inside, then the range man turned back into the saloon to carry the news that they wouldn't have to go on a manhunt, at least, because that feller who killed Bull Harris just entered the jailhouse with a couple of other fellows.

Rufe was wringing wet, but calm. He barred the door from inside, snarled for Ruff and Smith to back away, then got the cell-room keys and took his latest prisoners down to lock them into cells, also. Neither man offered so much as a single word of protest. Both of them knew a man primed to kill when they saw one.

Constable Bradshaw yelled at Rufe: "What was the shooting about? What the hell you and your partner done? By God, when we get out of here . . . !"

"Shut up!" snapped Rufe, glaring past the bars. Homer Bradshaw said no more, but the look of hatred and defiance upon his coarse face was an epitome of malevolence.

It was Matthew Reilly, from a seat upon the bunk in the adjoining cell, looking from Pete Ruff and old Abe Smith to Rufe, who seemed to be more worried than defiant. He did not make a sound, but Pete Ruff did. He peered out at Rufe as though sunlight pained his eyes, and swore.

Rufe ignored them all and returned to the front office, outward bound. He did not get very far. There was an angry crowd marching down the road from the direction of the saloon, some of them brandishing rifles.

Rufe looked around, found the gun rack, picked out a shotgun with a two-foot barrel, checked the breech, snapped the gun closed, and stepped back to the window. He had no intention of hurting anyone. All he wanted was a way out, so that he could find Jud.

On the rear skirts of that angry mob the old man in

the long coat was shuffling along, happy as a clam and grinning from ear to ear. He did not have a gun in sight, but he had a half-empty quart bottle of some-one's whiskey clutched in one of his mottled talons.

There were range men in the front of the crowd, but it consisted mostly of townsmen in shoes in-stead of boots. The range men halted at the tie rack, in tree shade, looked steadily at the brick wall, and called for Rufe to come out.

Rufe eased the double-barrels around into sight. Someone saw them, squawked like a wounded ea-gle, and men scattered every which way except for a grizzled, hard-looking old cattleman, and all he did was lean down upon the tie rack flintily staring back. He hardly more than raised his voice when he said: "What the hell you figure to do with that silly thing, cowboy? It don't have a range of over a hun-nert and fifty feet." He spat, then said: "You better come out of there. So far, you ain't done nothing that maybe should have been done long ago. Bull Har-ris's no loss. But you shoot anyone else, and that's going to make a heap of difference, so you'd better just walk out of there."

Rufe listened, and pondered, then called back: "I got a better idea, mister, *you* come inside!"

The old stockman chewed, spat, looked left and right where the wary crowd was beginning to creep up again, then he said: "All right, I'll come inside. But I got to warn you . . . we got a constable here in Clearwater, and, as soon as folks can find him, he'll be along to arrest you."

Rufe stepped to the door, raised the bar, and opened the panel a crack. "Come in," he called. "And don't any of you other fellers move!"

The cowman turned, said something gruffly to a

range man nearby, then stepped around the tie rack bound for the jailhouse door.

Rufe pulled the door open a little wider, then slammed it behind the stockman, dropped the bar back into place one handed, and cocked the near barrel of his scatter-gun. "Put your six-gun on the desk," he ordered.

The old cowman obeyed, and stood a moment looking at the other two guns already lying there. He turned his head. "This here weapon with the initials carved on the butt belongs to Constable Bradshaw."

Rufe gestured with the shotgun. "Go over yonder and sit down, mister. Yeah, that's the constable's gun. He's locked in a cell."

The cowman's jaw sagged. He stared for a moment, then turned and went to a wall bench, and eased down, still looking nonplussed.

Rufe put the scatter-gun atop the desk, also. It looked like a small arsenal with all those loaded weapons lying atop the litter of scattered papers on the desk. He then went to the water bucket, ladled up a dipper full, and deeply drank, with the old range man watching his every move. When he finished and dropped the dipper back into the bucket, he wiped his face with a soiled sleeve, jerked up a chair, swung it, and sat down astraddle the chair facing the cowman.

XIV

It did not take as long to tell the cowman the entire story as it might have, and, by the time the cowman had heard it all, his weathered, craggy features had settled into a fresh series of lines.

His name was Evart Hartman. He was a widower with two grown sons running the cow outfit with him. It had been his sons out there, on either side of him at the tie rack. They were still out there.

Hartman gazed at Rufe, after he knew the entire story, and said: "I hope for your sake you've told me the truth."

Rufe shrugged that off. "Why should it make any difference now? None of you lowland cowmen would do a damned thing to help Elisabeth Cane before."

The cowman considered that for a moment without replying, then he changed the subject. "Got any objection to me seeing Homer Bradshaw?"

Rufe arose and went for the keys. He had no objections. He did not believe the constable would tell Evart Hartman the truth, but he had no objections to them talking, so he mutely escorted Hartman down into the cell room, and, when Hartman halted out front of the cell and Constable Bradshaw saw him, the cowman surprised Rufe. He said: "Homer, you always was a cheatin', underhanded feller."

Bradshaw sneered. "Why, because I was always a better man than your sons, Evart?"

Hartman's tough gaze drifted past and came to rest on Matthew Reilly. He wagged his head at Reilly. "I told you last year, Matt. I told you not to get involved with anything Homer worked up. Didn't I tell you that?"

Matthew Reilly arose from the side of his bunk, came forward, and gripped the bars along the front of the cell. "They was strays, Mister Hartman."

The cowman gazed stonily at Reilly without speaking, then turned and looked in at Pete Ruff and Abe Smith. He knew Ruff, but not Abe Smith, and all he actually knew of Pete Ruff was that he was range boss for Arlen Chase. He did not speak to Ruff. They looked steadily at one another until old Abe Smith bleated a plea, and Hartman glanced from Ruff to the old *cocinero*.

Old Abe Smith bewailed the unkind fate which had landed him there, loudly lamented his complete innocence, and, when Evart Hartman asked him what he did for Chase, Abe told him.

"*Cocinero* is all. I swear to you, mister, I never even so much as brang in the saddle stock in the morning. Alls I ever done was the cooking. And they never told me a blessed thing. Never confided in me at all. Alls I did was slave over that gawd-damned cook stove from dawn until dark, and got treated like I was a. . . ."

"If you worked on my outfit," stated Evart Hartman, breaking across Smith's running flow of words, "and talked this much, we'd hang you just plumb out of hand."

Hartman turned for a final face-off with Homer Bradshaw. "I been saying it for years, Homer. You always were an underhanded feller."

"I'm the law here!" exclaimed Bradshaw, glaring.

Hartman was not very impressed. "I'll go around town and see about that, now. You been running out o' rope for a long while, Homer."

Rufe, who had not said a word, accompanied the old cowman back to the office, locked the cell-room door, and pitched the ring of keys over atop all those weapons on the desk.

"Well?" he said to Hartman.

"Seems to me someone's got to find your partner and Arlen Chase," stated Hartman. "Also seems to me someone's got to ride atop the mesa and get Elisabeth Cane's side of all this." Hartman fished for his makings and stood, stooped and thoughtful, while Rufe went to the roadway windows and looked out. The crowd was still out there, but its mood had changed, which perhaps was inevitable. No one could stand around in the hot roadway being consistently angry or excited or indignant, whatever had motivated most of those men.

A number of men were idly standing over in front of the general store, talking. Others were southward and northward, but on the same, opposite, side of the road, also idly talking. The men out front, at the tie rack and in the vicinity of it, were mostly stockmen who were so accustomed to the heat they did not appear to be aware of it.

Rufe turned when the old cowman spoke through a thin drift of fragrant smoke.

"Where do you reckon them two went . . . Chase and your partner?"

Rufe had absolutely no idea. The last he had seen,

Jud had just punched Arlen Chase through the doors of the saloon, and had jumped out behind him. There had been no gunfire, no great shouts by either man, but, of course, there had been the stunning aftermath of his shoot-out with Bull Harris to interfere with his own, and everyone else's concern, about Jud and Arlen Chase.

He told the cowman that, if he could keep the townsmen and those range men out there as well from interfering, he would try and locate his partner. Hartman smoked, and thought, and finally said: "I'll go with you." He did not explain why he would do this, and Rufe, eyeing the shrewd older man, felt that he understood. Evart Hartman was not an incautious man. He had seemed entirely convinced by the story Rufe had told him. In the cell room his attitude had reinforced Rufe's feeling that this was indeed so. On the other hand, Hartman's offer to accompany Rufe was not based entirely upon a desire to help. He wanted to be along just in case all his partial convictions turned out to be incorrect. He looked like that kind of a man, shrewd, careful, completely and analytically poised.

Rufe went to the desk, picked up Hartman's weapon, and handed it to him, then he motioned toward the door, and Hartman crossed over as he holstered his weapon. When he stood in the doorway, looking out, he spoke to the cowmen at the tie rack, but the moment that jailhouse door had opened, all those other men up and down the roadway, and upon the opposite plank walk, came straight up to listen.

Hartman was brusque. "Homer Bradshaw's locked in a cell in here, boys, along with Matt Reilly and a couple of Arlen Chase's men . . . his range boss is one of 'em. Those rumors we been pickin' up around town now and then about Chase making trouble for old Amos Cane's girl atop the mesa been pretty much true. This feller in here with me, Rufe Miller, and his partner, the feller who's missing along with Arlen Chase, work for Miz Cane. Me and this feller are going to ride out and see if we can't find his partner and Chase. Someone'd ought to set here in the jailhouse and mind the town, and make certain none of the prisoners in here gets loose."

Hartman did not ask for volunteers. He pointed over the heads of the men nearest him to a portly, dark-haired man over in front of the general store. "You, Lemuel. You're head of the town council this year, and you got a clerk in the store to mind the business. You better come over here and ramrod this matter, because, sure as hell, Clearwater don't have any law at all right now."

Hartman dropped his arm, watched the distant storekeeper a moment to see whether he would agree, would start across toward the jailhouse, then called to Rufe to come out.

No one said a word. No one more than shuffled his feet a little when Rufe came forth from the jailhouse, until he was fully out there on the plank walk, then the old man in the long coat, still clutching someone's whiskey bottle, reared up from along the north doorways and said: "You sure done a job that's been a long while finding someone to do it, sonny." He did not explain, but the assumption was that he had in mind the killing of Bull Harris.

Evart Hartman called to a range man. "Jamie, fetch my horse down to the livery barn, will you?"

He strolled along with Rufe, and, as they entered the shady area out front of the barn, Rufe recognized a heavy-set, unkempt-looking individual standing in the runway of the barn that he had seen earlier rattling the jailhouse door, then stamping off, cursing, because that door had been locked. It was the liveryman. He greeted Hartman and Rufe with a palpably false smile and turned to pace along with them until Rufe located his horse, then the liveryman offered to do the rigging. Rufe declined, did his own saddling and bridling. Then he leaned across the saddle seat and said: "Hour back, or more, you wanted to get inside the jailhouse, mister. I saw you up there shaking the door. Why?"

The liveryman's coarse, florid features creased up into a smile that nearly completely obscured small, porcine eyes. "Just lookin' for old Homer. Me and him usually share a cup of coffee in the morning. Been doin' that for years, me an' old Homer."

Rufe had a feeling about the liveryman, but he neither knew the man personally nor had anything except that small feeling, so he scooped up reins and led his horse out front.

They did not have to wait long. When Hartman's animal arrived, the cowboy who brought it looked closely at Rufe, but spoke to the old cowman. "You know what you're doing, Pa?"

Hartman smiled for the first time. "No," he told the young cowboy, "but that don't have to mean much. Mostly, in my lifetime, I've been doing things I wasn't sure about." His eye turned kindly. "You send your brother back to mind the ranch. You and the other boys hang around town until this here is settled, and don't fret about me."

For Rufe, the mystery of Jud's disappearance seemed to be a case of pursuit. It had seemed to be that ever since Rufe's last glimpse of his partner, lunging out through the saloon doorway behind Arlen Chase.

He knew that neither Jud nor Chase had fired a shot, because, thus far today, there had only been one gunshot around town—the one that had resulted in the death of Bull Harris. He also knew that Chase had the advantage of being familiar with Clearwater, while Jud was not. Also, Chase was familiar with the desert cow range on all sides of Clearwater.

Rufe led the way up the alley behind the livery barn, located the shed where he and Jud had put Ruff and Chase's *cocinero* down in the bootleg hole, and took Hartman inside, just in case Jud had returned to this place with Chase.

Hartman knew the hole. He said that just about everyone else in the countryside knew about it, and remembered the old-timer who had at one time made some of the finest whiskey in the entire territory down in that hole.

But neither Chase nor Jud was there.

Hartman, it turned out, was also very knowledgeable about the town. They made a very thorough and painstaking search of it—without turning up any sign of either Rufe's partner or Arlen Chase.

Hartman shook his head about this. "They ain't here. No way under the sun for 'em to be here, and us not have found them this morning."

Rufe considered, and decided that, if Jud had pursued Chase out of Clearwater, the most logical route for Chase to have taken would have been back in the direction of his camp atop of Cane's Mesa, because he would believe he had men up there to reinforce him.

There was another consideration. Whoever that had been hours earlier Rufe and Jud had seen coming down off the mesa in bright sunlight should by

now be fairly well along on their way to town—
which should put them between Chase, pursued by
Jud, and the top of the mesa.

He explained all this to Evart Hartman. The cowman stoically listened, then turned and without a
word led off back up toward the northwesterly desert
beyond Clearwater, tipping down his hat, now that
the full heat of hot daytime was over the land, and
even a wide hat brim did not help a lot, because brilliant sunshine bounced up off millions of mica parti-
cles in the soil and sand, but the hat brim was better
than no protection at all as they rode to the edge of
town, then headed forth into the desert.

Rufe sashayed back and forth, but, as Evart Hartman pointed out, there were always fresh-shod
horse tracks this close to Clearwater. Unless Jud's
animal had very unusual shoes, his tracks would be
indistinguishable from all those other tracks, and
Hartman was correct.

Rufe was anxious without being actually very worried. Jud was a man who a harsh existence had
formed to survive under almost all adverse conditions, but particularly under the variety of conditions
he was now involved in.

What puzzled Rufe was where Jud could have
gone in his pursuit of Arlen Chase, and, most of all,
it puzzled him that there had been no gunfire.

Of course, by now the pursuit could have put Jud
and Arlen Chase a considerable distance from town,
by now there could be gunshots, and no one would
hear them in Clearwater.

XV

Evart Hartman knew the countryside they were traversing even though he had never run his cattle this far west. He also recalled meetings with Amos Cane, and recounted a few of them as they rode upcountry. When Rufe chided him for doing nothing about conditions on the mesa, Hartman did not deny that he had heard talk around town; what he *did* deny was his right, or the right of anyone else, to go charging out over the countryside like some damned silly Don Quixote, trying to right wrongs which would turn out to be, in nine out of ten cases, pure gossip.

Of course, Rufe could have pursued this, could have shredded that argument to pieces, but right at the moment he needed Evart Hartman, and he did not care a damn about the things folks should have done.

They were a considerable distance from town. The buildings and rooftops were still abundantly discernible, but sounds were deadened by the distance, when Rufe made another wide pass from west to east, seeking fresh trails, and this time he found promising sign. Even the old cowman studied it with interest, and afterward raised his head to gaze up along the bluff faces toward the top out of Cane's Mesa.

"I expect we should have figured Arlen'd do that. Only place he figures to find friends."

Rufe had already considered this, and he had also considered something else—up ahead, there had been someone coming down off the mesa. Before Chase could race up there, he was going to encounter those other people.

The encounter evidently occurred while Rufe and Hartman were discussing the chances of Chase's reaching his cow camp with Jud on his trail. Suddenly, up ahead some distance, several men shouted indignant, but wholly indistinguishable, words. Rufe did not wait; he gigged his horse, and reined back and forth through the underbrush. Evart Hartman, some little distance rearward, loped ahead, too, but with caution, and also with a six-gun in his right fist.

They did not find the horsemen until someone up ahead heard them coming, and bellowed for his companions to get down, to get to cover.

Rufe halted in a long slide when he heard that outcry. He knew that voice. It belonged to horse-killing Charley Fenwick!

While Rufe puzzled over that, Evart Hartman walked his horse on up the last 100 feet, still holding his balanced pistol, looking ahead through the man-high underbrush, and said: "Seen anyone up there?"

Rufe hadn't. He was in the act of dismounting when someone up ahead through the underbrush hoorawed a loose horse. It was an old ruse, and, while it had undeniable benefits, it failed this morning simply because the hoorawed horse and the men who had sent it stampeding through the underbrush to stir up anyone who might be out there sent the horse in the wrong direction. They sent it stampeding due southward, while Rufe and Evart Hartman were not only more westerly, but they also happened to be almost as far northward as the hidden men with Charley Fenwick were—although neither Rufe nor Hartman knew that this was true, until that loose horse broke away and went charging southward.

Evart made a slight clucking sound, lowered his Colt, and made a motion for Rufe to follow him in absolute silence. They left their animals hidden in underbrush and zigzagged through thorny brush until old Hartman sank to one knee, head cocked, and motioned for Rufe to slip in beside him.

Up ahead, on their right, they could hear men mumbling. Rufe detected Fenwick's voice again, and shook his head. The last time he'd seen Fenwick the cowboy had been chained in Elisabeth Cane's barn.

Finally something occurred which helped explain what was happening on ahead through the underbrush. An angry voice, made sharp by someone's incensed condition, said: "What'n hell you'd let him get away for? He'll fetch up his partner and a lousy posse!"

Rufe and Hartman exchanged a look, then Hartman dropped low as another, less furious voice said: "Hurry up with the horses so's we can get out of here. He can't do anything by himself, anyway, and by the time he gets back. . . ." The rest of this remark was lost as the speaker either turned his back in the direction of the two listening men, or just let his words trail off.

Someone back where Rufe and Hartman had left

their horses made a mountain quail call. It was real-
istic enough, except that Rufe knew that call. He
tapped Hartman's shoulder, jerked his head, and
began withdrawing back in that direction.

Jud was down there, calmly smoking a cigarette,
when Rufe, leading the way, came around a tall,
thorny stand of underbrush. Jud gazed over, and
shook his head dolorously. "What took you so
damned long?" he querulously asked.

Rufe introduced Evart Hartman, and Jud nodded,
still looking irritable. When Rufe said—"What's going on up there?"—Jud answered almost laconically.

"I almost had Chase, when the whole blasted ball
of wax gave way. He rode up onto them."

Hartman interrupted. "Rode up onto who?"

"Elisabeth bringing Fenwick and the other one
with her down to town to the jailhouse." Jud
shrugged. "Just as well she never made it, eh? Anyway, Chase threw down on her. I saw that much,
but, before I could get any closer, Chase freed Fenwick, gave him her pistol, and handed her carbine to
the other feller . . . and, hell, I lost out."

Rufe was intrigued. "Where's Elisabeth now?"

"Up there," replied Jud, dropping his smoke to
stamp it out. "They got her for their hostage. That's
what I meant when I said the whole damned thing
come unraveled." He glanced at Hartman. "Any
more fellers on their way?"

The old cowman shook his head. "No. But there's
the three of us . . . and if all they got is three guns. . . ."

Jud studied the old cowman with a sour look,
then turned toward Rufe. "Maybe we can hold them
down while someone rides back for more men." He
pointed. "They can't use the trail up the slope." His

meaning was clear; that trail going up to the mesa was fully exposed.

Hartman did not appear very impressed. As he said, there were a dozen other routes away from this particular spot. Jud nodded. "Then it's up to us to hold 'em here, isn't it?"

They ventured again back through the underbrush until they were close enough to hear men working with livestock. Shortly now Arlen Chase and his riding crew would attempt to escape, and Jud, still showing monumental disgust, gestured. "If you fellers will slip around yonder, one to the west, one to the east, I'll drive in a couple of bullets from down here. That ought to make them defensive." He looked at Rufe. "Just remember, I'm down here, if you get to throwing lead."

If there was a better way, they did not see it right then, and because they did not seem to have very much time to accomplish their purpose before Chase and his riders made their break for it, Rufe turned away, as did Evart Hartman, leaving Jud standing morosely behind the big thorn-pin tree.

Rufe's course was not difficult. All he had to do was avoid contact with the underbrush, and watch where he stepped in order to avoid dry twigs underfoot. He could hear an occasional voice up ahead, where Chase and his men were getting organized, but he did not pay much attention until he was between them and the uphill road leading back atop Cane's Mesa. Then he began skulking in closer, hoping for a view of the secreted men with Arlen Chase. What he specifically wished to determine was where Elisabeth was. If there was to be a battle, he did not want her endangered if there was any way to avoid it.

Of course, there was no way to avoid it. When he finally caught a glimpse of movement through the lower limbs of underbrush, what he saw was three horses, saddled and being held by someone who he could not distinctly make out at all.

He shoved his Colt forward, wriggled in as close as he could at the base of a particularly hardy stand of buckbrush, allowed a full minute to pass, during which he thought Jud and the old cowman would be in place, then he sang out.

"Chase! Fenwick! We're on all sides of you!"

He had more to say, but a nervous trigger finger up through the brush fired a gun in the direction of Rufe's voice, and the bullet made a tearing sound, clearly audible, but two feet higher than where Rufe was lying.

Rufe held his fire, intending to sing out again. From off to the east, far out, Evart Hartman fired; at least that shot came from the area where Rufe was certain Hartman had gone, but otherwise there was no way for Rufe to be sure who had fired.

This second gunshot, though, stirred up a hornet's nest. Two pistols and a Winchester cut loose in the same direction as Hartman had fired from. Rufe pushed his six-gun ahead, aimed as best he could at the ground beneath where those three saddled horses were being held, and tugged off a shot.

The noise was bad enough, but when that slug tore into the gravelly hardpan, causing an eruption of flinty soil and sharp little bits of stone, which flew upwards, striking the nearest horse under the belly, the animal gave a tremendous bound into the air, and snorted like a wild stallion.

A man swore as the other two held horses also violently reacted, and another man yelled for the horse holder to hang on.

Rufe fired again in the same way, his bullet exploding hardpan upward beneath those terrified horses, and this time two furiously swearing men fired back as they rushed over to help the horse holder.

Both those last two bullets also went high above where Rufe was lying. Nevertheless, it would only be a matter of moments before Chase's riders figured out that Rufe was belly down out there. They would then lower their gun barrels, but right at this moment everyone through the brush was desperately seeking to control the frightened horses.

Rufe had no intention of allowing the men to get their animals under control, if he could help it. As long as they were fully occupied with their only means of escape, he was relatively safe from their wrath.

He wriggled away from his big bush and crept still closer. While he was crawling, Jud fired from southward, but high. So high, in fact, that the bullet clipped a dozen small branches from the tops of the bushes. Rufe saw this happen, saw the underbrush rip and tear as Jud's slug bore through it.

It occurred to him that Jud was also thinking of Elisabeth's safety, when he fired that high.

Rufe found another massive old bush, but when he pushed aside low branches to get into the protection of the trunk at ground level, he met an agitated rattlesnake, coiled in the shade to avoid the full day's heat. Rufe began carefully reversing himself, began to crawl backward as surely as, moments before, he had crawled forward.

Evidently the snake was as willing to have Rufe do that as Rufe was because he neither rattled nor raised his flat, ugly-snouted head.

Hartman fired again, and this time someone through the underbrush swore at the old cowman, then ripped off two very fast pistol shots.

Jud fired again, still high, and Rufe added another gunshot. This time, the men up ahead did not return Rufe's fire, and only one man let fly in Jud's direction, and he fired too far to the east to endanger Jud.

For a couple of minutes there was absolute silence. Evart Hartman, who had not said a word until now, called forth in a tone of voice that was almost too calm.

"Hey, you fellers! So far, you're not in any real bad trouble. At least, so far you ain't done anything folks'll want to hang you for. But you keep this up, and maybe hit someone, and you're going to end up out back of the livery barn at the end of a rope. You sure it's worth it?"

The silence continued after Hartman had called out. Rufe was hopeful. The long silence encouraged him in this. He reasoned that, if Chase's crew was really fired up to kill, one or the other of them, at least, would have answered the cowman with gunshots.

Finally a voice Rufe knew belonged to Fenwick called out: "We'll make a trade with you fellers! We'll leave Miz Cane settin' here tied up, like she is, and we'll take the horses and head on out ... providin' you fellers agree not to shoot, and not to make an attempt to interfere with us getting away. All right?"

Rufe answered quickly: "Send Miz Cane southward on her own first."

For a moment there was no answer, then it came,

apparently after a heated discussion by the men hiding in the underbrush.

"We got a better notion. We'll take her along with us for a mile or two, just to keep you fellers honest, and, if you don't go and try to interfere with us heading out, we'll set her loose. And that's the only terms we'll talk about, so you either agree or don't agree."

Rufe sighed, waited for Jud or Evart Hartman to speak, and after a minute, when neither of them had made a sound, Rufe called out agreement to the terms.

XVI

Those agitated saddle animals were perfectly willing to settle down, once the gunfire ended. Rufe could see men's legs in among the horses, but that was about all he could see, until two men brought up a third person. He recognized the high-topped dark boots and the riding skirt of Elisabeth Cane, and watched as Chase's men put her astride one of the horses, then, by pulling back a few yards and peering over the tops of the tallest bushes, he could see her head and shoulders.

They had bound her arms behind her back, but with a short length of rope hanging loosely enough so that she had a little room to move her wrists, which struck Rufe as a charitable thing to do.

She sat her horse, looking scornfully around where the men were completing their arrangements to get astride, then she turned, looked over the tops of the bushes—and saw Rufe. He smiled and winked. She winked back, but did not smile, and a moment later she looked dead ahead, southward, as though she had seen nothing.

She looked regal, up there atop that horse, shoulders squared, head tilted just a little, her firm mouth set in an expression of acceptance without compromise. Rufe thought again that she was an unusually handsome woman, then a dry voice called from the east, but much closer than the same voice had sounded earlier, as Evart Hartman addressed Arlen Chase.

"As a matter of curiosity, Arlen," said Hartman. "If you run for Mexico, you're leavin' an awful lot behind. If I was in your boots, I'd face it . . . and at least salvage something."

It struck Rufe as good advice. Perhaps it also struck Arlen that way, but he certainly gave no indication of it. He did not respond at all, and moments later Rufe could see them getting astride.

They acted wary, once they were exposed atop their horses. It was an understandable reaction, only moments earlier they had been shooting at the unseen watchers around them, and those same watchers had been shooting back. Now they were sitting ducks, except that a verbal agreement had been reached. The men had guns in their hands and kept casting glances around, somewhat fearfully, as though they expected to see a gun barrel aimed their way.

The last man up held a Colt that looked very new. The bluing was not rubbed off in any place that Rufe could see. Rufe watched as this man looked left, then right. While he was facing in Hartman's direction, he said: "Why are you worrying about what I'm leaving behind, Hartman, if you didn't have some notion of comin' up here after I'm gone, like a lousy vulture, and gleaning everything that isn't tied down?"

Hartman was an honest man. "I had something like that in mind," he admitted calmly. "Only I don't steal, Arlen. I had in mind rounding up the stock I might want, then finding whoever represented you, and buying it from 'em."

"You can buy it from me," stated Arlen Chase, and the dry answer he got back indicated just how far old Hartman's opinion of Chase had sunk this morning.

"I wouldn't buy an old trade blanket from you, Arlen."

Fenwick urged his horse up beside Chase's, leaned and growled something. Chase nodded, turned away from Hartman, and gestured for the little band to move out.

Rufe stepped back, got clear of the brush, then trotted down to where his horse was. When he arrived there, Jud was already snugging up a cinch on the animal he had led up from a more distant hiding place. They were listening to the progress of Chase's band moving through underbrush when Evart Hartman came up, panting. He grabbed the reins Jud offered, climbed up across leather without testing the cinch, and hauled his animal around just in time for them to be able to hear the riders to the east of them, moving over in the direction of the stage road, although Rufe did not believe Chase would actually go that far east. And he didn't. When Hartman, Jud, and Rufe angled so as to stay behind the retreating riders, it became clear that Chase was paralleling the road, but was not going to make an attempt actually to reach and use it.

Rufe was speculating aloud with Jud and Evart Hartman what Chase's course would be when they got down closer to Clearwater, and got his answer in a way neither he nor the men with him expected. Two riders appeared coming upcountry from the direction of town. They had evidently been instructed about where to abandon the roadway and head into the desert, because, although they were heading in the correct direction, they seemed quite unconvinced of it, right up until the moment someone riding with Arlen Chase called out a warning, and Chase reined over close to Elisabeth Cane, then looked all around before spotting the oncoming men.

Rufe saw no one. Neither did Jud, but old Evart Hartman had picked up a fresh presence from his horse, and was riding along, watching intently over easterly in the direction of the stage road. He did not actually see those two men, but ultimately heard them coming, heard Chase's man growl, and finally, standing in his stirrups, he saw something that could have been fresh horsemen passing in and out among the southerly undergrowth. When old Hartman settled back down in his saddle and leaned slightly to tell Rufe what was down there, someone fired a pistol.

It was an unexpected sound. It not only startled every man; it also made the horses of Rufe and Jud and Evart Hartman throw up their heads. Dead ahead, Rufe heard Fenwick cry out in protest, and then the other one in Chase's party started to yell, but without warning another gunshot rang out, then a third and fourth gunshot erupted.

Hartman grunted and hauled his mount around to spur eastward. The same singing lead coming up-country had similarly inspired Rufe and Jud to get clear. They were riding low in the saddle, peering back in the direction of those gunshots, when a powerful sorrel horse suddenly plowed through a stand of brush heading arrow straight right at Rufe and Jud.

They had about four seconds to adjust to being attacked, and fortunately they were already looking in that direction, so the plunging horse did not catch them entirely unaware. The animal was gathering momentum each time it sank its hind hoofs down after bursting through the underbrush. Within another ten or fifteen yards, the horse would be running belly down straight toward the old trail up to the mesa.

Rufe yelped and Jud swung wide to allow the sorrel to come in between them, its reins flopping wildly from a looped position over the saddle horn. There was no way for the rider, with both arms bound behind her back, to control the running horse, except in a very unreliable way through knee pressure. How she had turned and got free, Rufe did not dwell on as he jumped his horse out to come in running beside the big sorrel. Leather strained, stirrups grated together, and Elisabeth's face was close enough for Rufe to see the fear in her dark eyes when he leaned far out to grab for the reins under the sorrel's jaw.

On the far side, Jud, aware of his partner's intention, made no attempt to grab reins, but he leaned his own straining mount into the sorrel on Elisabeth's left side, forcing her horse over against Rufe's animal. That way, Rufe was able to get a double hold on the reins, and ease back, bringing both horses down to a jarring, slamming halt.

He looked at Elisabeth. She showed a shaky small smile as Jud moved in with his clasp knife to free her arms. As he reached for the rope, Jud said: "How did you get away?"

Her answer was a surprise. "I didn't. One of the men turned my horse and struck it over the rump, when that shooting started. The horse was heading straight for the trail up to my home atop the mesa." She smiled with more confidence as she brought her arms in front and massaged chapped wrists. "It would have been a rather terrifying ride."

Jud pocketed his knife and turned as a man's gruff voice called. It was Hartman calling to them, but for a moment the voice did not sound exactly right.

"Rufe . . . Jud! Come on down here! The whole damned story's been wrote out and ended! Fetch the lady back with you, and come on down here! See for yourselves!"

They went carefully and prudently, with Elisabeth remaining slightly to the rear, but their precautions proved unnecessary. Evart Hartman did not even have a gun in his hand where he sat atop his horse, gazing at something out of sight in the underbrush. Charley Fenwick did not have a gun in his hand, nor did the other two men with Charley, the same men Rufe finally remembered now and was able to identify. At least, he could identify their faces, although he had never met either of them, or heard their names. It was the same two men Jud and Rufe had seen walk out of the abstract office down in Clearwater, vigorously talking to Arlen Chase.

There was one man on foot, and this man had a pistol in his hand. He was the older cowboy Rufe and Jud had left chained in Elisabeth Cane's barn along with Fenwick. But he simply stood there, staring.

Rufe did not see Arlen Chase until he and Jud eased around the underbrush to come up beside old Hartman. Chase was dead. It looked as though two bullets had hit him, both of them striking his chest. Impact had knocked him backward from the saddle. He was being held in a grotesque sitting posture by the strong and wiry limbs of the bush he had tumbled into.

Elisabeth looked once, then turned away. Even tough Jud did not like that look of entreaty, or supplication, or whatever it was that seemed to emanate from the corpse, from the way it was held up like that, in a begging posture. Jud turned away, too, but not entirely from revulsion. He eyed the pair of strangers and said: "Who shot him?"

One of the newcomers answered. "I did. He shot at us when we started through the underbrush toward him. I shot back, then my partner here, also fired back. We nailed him."

Jud showed no particular remorse, but he frowned. "Why, stranger, why would he shoot at you?"

The horseman gazed around from face to face, before answering Jud, and even then his answer was not very satisfactory. "It's a long tale, friend. We'll be glad to explain it fully, back in Clearwater, to the proper authorities."

Rufe frowned a little. "Mister, for now, you can just sort of pretend we're the proper authorities."

Both the strangers looked entirely able to care for themselves. Neither one of them quailed the least bit under Rufe's mildly unpleasant stare, but one of them, the man who took the blame—or credit—for downing Arlen Chase, looked back at the dead man, evidently completely unimpressed by the corpse's posture, and said: "That man, gents, sold my brother and me six thousand acres atop a mesa in this here country, when we met him a couple of months back over in Nogales, while we were looking around for some grazing land. Then we came up here to look over what we'd bought, and the old feller at the abstract office told us, just this damned morning, that the title and deed to that land atop this here mesa was legally vested in a woman named Elisabeth Cane. We told Mister Chase we wanted our money back . . . or the deed to the mesa, free and clear, and he told us in the saloon, back there in town, he'd get it for us by tomorrow. That he'd deliver the deed as heir to Cane's Mesa. And after that, when all hell busted loose down in town, and he lit out, we figured we'd best light out, too, in order kind of to protect our investment. Some fellers around the livery barn told us how to reach the mesa. We was heading up there, when this happened." The stranger gestured toward the corpse in the bushes. "The damned fool shot at us when he saw us passing through the underbrush." The stranger stopped speaking and gazed around.

It was Chase's man, Charley Fenwick, who threw up his arms. "Gawd damn it," he cried in exasperation. "First it was just her horses, then just her cattle, then it was burn her out . . . now this." Fenwick looked at the man with the pistol hanging at his side, the other man Rufe and Jud had left chained in the barn. The cowboy looked back at Fenwick, and slowly leathered his weapon, turned just as slowly to mount his horse, and finally he spoke.

"I told you and Pete Ruff, consarn it, Charley. I been tellin' you pair of idiots for the past three, four months, he was gettin' us all in deeper and deeper."

Jud pointed to the corpse and gave an order to the man who had just mounted his horse. "Get down, mister, fling Chase over his horse, lash him to it, and lead him on down to town." Jud's uncompromising look inspired the cowboy to obey.

Watching the cowboy work and looking as uncompromising as ever, Jud added a little more to what he had already said: "That lousy jailhouse down in Clearwater's going to be full to the rafters." He looked at Evart Hartman. "You reckon there's enough honest folks down there to set up some kind of law court?"

Evart's answer was cryptic. "You can bet new money on it."

Jud looked at Rufe, eyebrows raised. Rufe looked at Elisabeth. "Ought to be getting' back to the ranch," he told her, and she, too, looked at Evart Hartman. This time, the old cowman did not wait to be addressed. He smiled at the handsome woman.

"Looks to me like we sort of owe you something, Miz Cane. I'll send word out that we'll need maybe ten, fifteen good range riders to help scour the desert and fetch back to your mesa all the Lance-and-Shield livestock we can find. All right, ma'am?"

Elisabeth avoided watching Arlen Chase being lashed limply, belly down, across his saddle when she replied to Hartman. "All right, Mister Hartman. But I don't need charity."

The old cowman squinted a moment, then glanced at Rufe, slightly raising and lowering his shoulders as though to say: *What the hell can you do with a female like this?*

XVII

It was in Rufe's thoughts that they should have ridden back to Clearwater to make certain justice was done. It was also in his mind that Evart Hartman, now that he was convinced that Arlen Chase had been everything honest livestock men disapproved of—horse thief, cattle rustler, land thief—would grimly make a particular point of seeing that justice was done.

Jud may have been thinking along these lines, too, because, as he and Rufe and Elisabeth Cane reached the trail leading upward to the mesa top, Jud said: "Folks just naturally shy clear of unpleasantness, and maybe that's how fellers like Chase manage to succeed. Seems to me, we'd ought to hang around, down there in Clearwater, and make blessed sure things come out right."

Elisabeth, who had been riding in silence most of the way, smiled at Jud. "It's a big country. There aren't many people in it, but once they know for a fact someone is stealing and lying, you can depend upon them to do whatever has to be done to put an end to it."

Rufe listened, and said nothing. As far as he was concerned, the case against Arlen Chase did not need any more proving, and with Chase dead, and his gunfighter dead, also, and his cowboys like Fenwick and that older rider willing to tell what they knew, there would be justice. Belated justice, for a fact—Matt Reilly, Constable Bradshaw, and another rider, the one who had taken his money from the stolen horses and gone back to Texas with it—had seriously crippled Elisabeth's cow outfit, but even that was not beyond repair.

He eyed Elisabeth thoughtfully. "Did Chase have pretty fair quality cattle, ma'am?"

"Yes. He had scrubs, like everyone else, but his grade stock was fair quality. Why?"

Rufe glanced up the trail they were riding as he said: "Well, a funny thing crossed my mind just now. Arlen Chase's mark was AC. And seems to me someone said your pappy's name was Amos Cane, and that figures out AC, too."

Elisabeth's dark eyes widened on Rufe. He knew exactly what she was thinking, but he hadn't mentioned any of this with any thought in mind of stealing AC cattle, so he explained. "Suppose you could borrow some money, maybe from local stockmen like old Hartman, or maybe from some bank, if there is one in the country. Why, then, you could buy Chase's iron . . . the AC . . . and that way you'd acquire his livestock, and, if you'd care to reregister his iron in your pappy's name, why then we wouldn't have all that re-branding to do. You'd have two irons, AC and your Lance-and-Shield brand."

Even Jud, after some thought about this, smiled a little. He winked at Elisabeth, then spoke to his partner. "Every once in a while you do come up with something that could pass for a smart idea. Not often, but every now and then."

They reached the top out, passed silently through

the abandoned cow camp of the defunct Arlen Chase, and hardly a word more passed among the three of them until, with the sun angling away westerly, they had the rooftop of the old log barn in sight, and this reminded Jud of something.

"Ma'am, how come you to unchain those fellers we left in your barn?"

"I was going to take them down to Clearwater and sign a warrant against them at the jailhouse." She looked sharply at Jud, when he sighed loudly over this statement, then waggled his head. "What's wrong with that, Jud?"

"Nothing much, ma'am, except that one of the fellers who was involved in stealing and selling your livestock was the town marshal of Clearwater."

Elisabeth looked at Rufe, who gravely nodded his head, then she said: "I didn't have any idea Homer Bradshaw was involved. No idea at all."

Jud was able to be charitable in the face of her ignorance, because he was more interested in something else. "He was, and that's a plumb fact. Now tell me, ma'am, how did those fellers manage to turn on you?"

"We were going down the trail. It didn't seem decent to me to make them ride chained like that. They couldn't control their horses, or even. . . ."

"So you took off the chains," muttered Jud, and rolled up his eyes. "I reckon it's true, what we heard about handsome females, Rufe. If they got looks, they don't have much in the way of brains."

Elisabeth reddened and her eyes sparked, but she simply rode along, watching Jud roll a smoke, and kept all her quick, biting comments in check.

Rufe leaned, touched her hand atop the saddle horn, and said: "That was a compliment."

If this ameliorated Elisabeth's annoyance, it did not show until they reached the barn and off-saddled out front, then, as she turned to head for the main house to prepare supper, she smiled very sweetly at Jud.

"There is something I've always heard, too, Jud . . . that, if a cowboy is worth his salt, he'll never quit, once he's hired on, just because an outfit is in trouble. When will you be riding on?"

They both leaned on the tie rack, watching her walk toward the house. Jud removed his hat, scratched his head, replaced the hat with indifferent aim, and screwed up his face toward Rufe. "What in hell did she mean by that? It sounded like she figured me to be one of those rolling stones, or something."

Rufe side-stepped a direct answer as he led his horse and Elisabeth's sorrel over to a corral and put them inside. Jud came along later, and did the same thing, then the pair of them met inside where they forked some hay to the horses, and Jud was still puzzled.

"She don't like me," he told Rufe. "She don't want me around. I think that's what she meant."

Rufe said: "Naw, she was just answering back for what you said about beautiful women being dumb, in the way womenfolk get back at men."

Jud still did not understand, but he eventually gave up even trying when they caught the smell of cooking food in the evening air. Jud stood in the barn doorway, looking in the direction of the house, faintly scowling. "Well, hell," he said plaintively, "no woman that handsome has to have brains, too, does she?"

Rufe agreed. "She sure don't." He looked out

across the night-shadowed mesa. "We'd ought to stay up here, Jud. Get the ranch back on its feet, anyway."

Jud put a wryly wise look upon his partner. "Sure. And that's the only reason you'd want to stay here for a few years. Couldn't have anything to do with the look in her eyes when she smiles at you, or that sick-calf look you get when you smile back." Jud snorted and hauled up. "I got to go wash at the creek and slick down my hair. Don't seem decent, a friend of yours lookin' like the backend of a bear when he's set-tin' at the same supper table with you and her . . . whilst you're exchanging those calf-eyed looks."

Jud struck out in the direction of the creek, leaving Rufe where he was, in front of the barn, softly gazing in the direction of the lighted main house windows.

For a fact she was a beautiful woman. A man could ride two-thirds of his entire lifetime and never see another woman that handsome. And this mesa was one hell of a long way from the Gila Valley, too.

About the Author

Lauran Paine who, under his own name and various pseudonyms has written over 1,000 books, was born in Duluth, Minnesota, a distant descendant of the Revolutionary War patriot and author, Thomas Paine. His family moved to California when he was at a young age and his apprenticeship as a Western writer came about through the years he spent in the livestock trade, rodeos, and even motion pictures where he served as an extra because of his expert horsemanship in several films starring movie cowboy Johnny Mack Brown. In the late 1930s, Paine trapped wild horses in northern Arizona and even, for a time, worked as a professional farrier. Paine came to know the Old West through the eyes of many who had been born in the previous century, and he learned that Western life had been very different from the way it was portrayed on the screen. "I knew men who had killed other men," he later recalled. "But they were the exceptions. Prior to and during the Depression, people were just too busy eking out an existence to indulge in Saturday-night brawls." He served in the U.S. Navy in the Second World War and began writing for Western pulp magazines following his discharge. It is interesting to note that all of his earliest novels (written under his own name and the pseudonym Mark Carrel) were published in the British market and he soon had as strong a following in that country as in the United States. Paine's Western fiction is characterized by strong plots, authenticity, an apparently effortless ability to construct situation and character, and a preference for building his stories upon a solid foundation of historical fact. *Adobe Empire* (1956), one of his best novels, is a fictionalized account of the last twenty years in the life of trader William Bent and, in an off-trail way, has a melancholy, bittersweet texture that is not easily forgotten. In later novels like *The White Bird* and *Cache Cañon*, he has shown that the special magic and power of his stories and characters have only matured along with his basic themes of changing times, changing attitudes, learning from experience, respecting Nature, and the yearning for a simpler, more moderate way of life.

COTTON SMITH

"Cotton Smith is one of the finest of a new breed of writers of the American West."

—Don Coldsmith

Return of the Spirit Rider

In the booming town of Denver, saloon owner Vin Lockhart is known as a savvy businessman with a quick gun. But he will never forget that he was raised an Oglala Sioux. So when Vin's Oglala friends needed help dealing with untruthful, encroaching white men, he swore he would do what he could. His dramatic journey will include encounters with Wild Bill Hickok and Buffalo Bill Cody. But when an ambush leaves him on the brink of death, his only hope is what an old Oglala shaman taught him long ago.

"Cotton Smith is one of the best new authors out there."

—Steven Law, Read West

ISBN 13: 978-0-8439-5854-6

ANDREW J. FENADY

Owen Wister Award-Winning Author of *Big Ike*

No mission is too dangerous as long as the cause—and the money—are right. Four soldiers of fortune, along with a beautiful woman, have crossed the Mexican border to dig up five million dollars in buried gold. But between the Trespassers and their treasure lie a merciless comanchero guerilla band, a tribe of hostile Yaqui Indians and Benito Juarez's army. It's a journey no one with any sense would hope to survive, or would even dare to try, except...

The Trespassers

Andrew J. Fenady is a Spur Award finalist and recipient of the prestigious Owen Wister Award for his lifelong contribution to Western literature, and the Golden Boot Award, in recognition of his contributions to the Western genre. He has written eleven novels and numerous screenplays, including the classic John Wayne film *Chisum*.

ISBN 13: 978-0-8439-6024-2

"When you think of the West, you think of Zane Grey." —*American Cowboy*

ZANE GREY

THE RESTORED, FULL-LENGTH NOVEL,
IN PAPERBACK FOR THE FIRST TIME!

The Great Trek

Sterl Hazelton is no stranger to trouble. But the shooting that made him an outlaw was one he didn't do. Though it was his cousin who pulled the trigger, Sterl took the blame, and now he has to leave the country if he wants to stay healthy. Sterl and his loyal friend, Red Krehl, set out for the greatest adventure of their lives, signing on for a cattle drive across the vast northern desert of Australia to the gold fields of the Kimberley Mountains. But it seems no matter where Sterl goes, trouble is bound to follow!

"Grey stands alone in a class untouched by others." —*Tombstone Epitaph*

ISBN 13: 978-0-8439-6062-4

LOUIS L'AMOUR
TRAILING WEST

The Western stories of Louis L'Amour are loved the world over. His name has become synonymous with the West for millions of readers, as no other author has so brilliantly recreated that thrilling and unique era of American history. Here, collected together in paperback for the first time, are one of L'Amour's greatest novellas and three of his finest stories, all carefully restored to their original magazine publication versions.

The keystone of this collection, the novella *The Trail to Crazy Man*, features the courage and honor that characterize so much of L'Amour's best work. In it, Rafe Caradec heads out to Wyoming, determined to keep his word and protect the daughter of a dead friend from the man who wants to take her ranch—whether she wants his help or not. Each classic tale in this volume represents a doorway to the American West, a time of heroism and adventure, brought to life as only Louis L'Amour could do it!

ISBN 13: 978-0-8439-6067-9

To order a book or to request a catalog call:
1-800-481-9191

This book is also available at your local bookstore, or you can check out our Web site **www.dorchesterpub.com** where you can look up your favorite authors, read excerpts, or glance at our discussion forum to see what people have to say about your favorite books.

John D. Nesbitt

"John Nesbitt knows working cowboys and ranch life well enough for you to chew the dirt with his characters."
— *True West*

FIRST TIME IN PRINT!

Will Dryden picked the wrong time to ride onto the Redstone Ranch. He was looking for a job...and a missing man. But one of the Redstone's hands was just found killed, so tensions are riding high and not everyone's eager to welcome a stranger. The more questions Dryden asks, the more twisted everything seems, and the more certain he is that someone's got something to hide. Something worth killing for. Dryden just has to make sure he doesn't catch a bullet before he finds out what's behind all the...

TROUBLE AT THE REDSTONE

ISBN 13: 978-0-8439-6055-6

ROBERT J. CONLEY

FIRST TIME IN PRINT!

NO NEED FOR A GUNFIGHTER

"One of the most underrated and overlooked writers of our time, as well as the most skilled."
—Don Coldsmith, Author of the Spanish Bit Saga

BARJACK VS...EVERYBODY!

The town of Asininity didn't think they needed a tough-as-nails former gunfighter for a lawman anymore, so they tried—as nicely as they could—to fire Barjack. But Barjack likes the job, and he's not about to move on. With the dirt he knows about some pretty influential folks, there's no way he's leaving until he's damn good and ready. So it looks like it's the town versus the marshal in a fight to the finish... and neither side is going to play by the rules!

Conley is "in the ranks of N. Scott Momaday, Louise Erdrich, James Welch or W. P. Kinsella."
—*The Fort Worth Star-Telegram*

ISBN 13: 978-0-8439-6077-8

☐ **YES!**

Sign me up for the Leisure Western Book Club and send my FREE BOOKS! If I choose to stay in the club, I will pay only $14.00* each month, a savings of $9.96!

NAME: _____

ADDRESS: _____

TELEPHONE: _____

EMAIL: _____

☐ I want to pay by credit card.

☐ **VISA**   ☐ MasterCard.   ☐ DISCOVER

ACCOUNT #: _____

EXPIRATION DATE: _____

SIGNATURE: _____

Mail this page along with $2.00 shipping and handling to:
Leisure Western Book Club
PO Box 6640
Wayne, PA 19087
Or fax (must include credit card information) to:
610-995-9274
You can also sign up online at **www.dorchesterpub.com**.

*Plus $2.00 for shipping. Offer open to residents of the U.S. and Canada only. Canadian residents please call 1-800-481-9191 for pricing information.

If under 18, a parent or guardian must sign. Terms, prices and conditions subject to change. Subscription subject to acceptance. Dorchester Publishing reserves the right to reject any order or cancel any subscription.